I0640718

John G Beane

Cardinal Lavigerie

Primate of Africa

John G Beane

Cardinal Lavigerie
Primate of Africa

ISBN/EAN: 9783741190056

Manufactured in Europe, USA, Canada, Australia, Japa

Cover: Foto ©Andreas Hilbeck / pixelio.de

Manufactured and distributed by brebook publishing software
(www.brebook.com)

John G Beane

Cardinal Lavigerie

CONTENTS.

THE LIFE

OF

CARDINAL LAVIGERIE,

THE PRIMATE OF AFRICA.

CHAPTER I.

BIRTH OF CHARLES LAVIGERIE, HIS COLLEGE LIFE AND ECCLESIASTICAL VOCATION.

Fifty years ago the history of the African Continent might be expressed in a few words : A brief outline of Egypt from the pages of the Bible ; the Cape of Good Hope, which was discovered in 1496 by Bartholomew Dias, and doubled in 1497 by Vasco de Gama; and the traces of African civilization as found in the history of the ancient Roman Empire. But now Africa is a more intricate study, and classed as it is with modern discoveries, it has attracted the attention of the nineteenth century ; and Timbuctoo, Sakhala, Khartum, Zanzibar and the other centres of African civilization have become sources of wealth to European governments. Curious and intrepid travelers have penetrated the wilds of Africa, and have opened the country to commerce ; whilst zealous and God-fearing missioners have labored for the conversion of the idolatrous Mussulmans, and have brought to light the horrors of that traffic of Negro slavery which stains with human blood the land of equatorial Africa.

Amongst the courageous men who have devoted their time, talents, energy and life to the alleviation of oppressed and unfortunate Africa was Cardinal Lavigerie, the Primate of Africa and Archbishop of Carthage and Algiers. Charles Martial Allemand Lavigerie was born at Bayonne, France, October 31, 1825. His mother's family came from the Lower Provinces; hence, on the maternal side he was associated with the country of such apostles as St. Ignatius and St. Francis Xavier; and although in character, sympathy and sentiment he was French, yet he felt the influence of that maternal blood which characterized his actions even when he became Cardinal.

He was the eldest of four children, and he received the first principles of religion from his father, who carefully guarded over the spiritual welfare of his little flock. He had the happiness of receiving his first holy Communion from Father Franchisteguy, afterwards the Vicar General to Bishop Lacroix of Bayonne, and the example and direction of this pious and enlightened priest gave a recruit to the army of Christ. Charles revealed to his parents his desire of becoming a priest, but they strongly opposed him, for, as he was the eldest of the family, his father desired him to embrace an honorable, but a worldly, career. The thought of holy orders was repulsive, for it meant a more complete separation from family ties than the career of the magistrate or the lawyer.

Such is the heart of parents; they place the first obstacle in the path of their children, although they rejoice at the final decision of a vocation. When a terrestrial union is sought, the most prudent parents willingly risk their own and their children's welfare in the hope of a human happiness; but when God makes the demand they pause—their long experience is not sufficient to decide a matter of so grave importance. The delay with Charles lasted a a year and a half, during which time he was severely tried, but his firmness surmounted every obstacle. At last his father presented him to the Bishop, whose kindness made a deep impression on him who one day would be a prince of the Church. "I have always before me," he writes, "the spacious room of the Bishop, the yellow velvet furniture, the chair in which he was seated, and the purple cassock which he wore. My heart beat very quickly, but he soon placed me at my ease." Yet that heart which was so terrified in the presence of the Bishop was a valiant heart, and it contained the most necessary sacerdotal virtues—humility, detachment, and freedom from human ambition.

The Bishop perceived the latent virtues of the young man, and his Spanish imagination yielded perhaps to a transient enthusiasm or to an ambitious dream. "He drew me towards him," says Lavigerie, "and he caressed me with his venerable hands, and he said to me: "So you have, my child, a vocation to the priesthood?" "Yes, Bishop," I replied. "And why do you wish to be a priest?" he asked. "In order that I may have a country parish," I answered. My father was astonished, for he did not know that I had such rural tastes, but the Bishop, smilingly, said to me: "You will go to the Seminary of Larresorre, and then you will be whatever God wishes."

What a profound word—you will be whatever God wishes!
He had clearly seen my destiny.   I went to the Seminary
of Larresorre, but afterwards whither does my path lead?
Amid the agitations and the fatigues of my life my country parish has remained the dream of my youth and sometimes the regret of my mature age.   God has led me
whither He willed, as Bishop Lacroix had predicted, and
so to-day I am writing, not from a country parish, but
from the ruins of Carthage."

Thirty-six years after this conversation between the
Bishop and the youth, Bishop Lacroix and Father
Franchisteguy were one day walking on the seashore
near the mouth of the Adour river.   An old man with a
long white beard who appeared fatigued by labor, care
and the rigors of a burning climate, joined them; he was
Bishop Lavigerie, the little Charles of former days.   God
had led him whither He wished, and He had wished him
Primate of Africa and Archbishop of Algiers.   There he
was, aged before his time, between the Bishop who had
confirmed him and the priest from whom he had received
his first Communion.   He remarked with a touch of sadness that he had a more aged appearance than had his
former masters.   "Why," replied Bishop Lacroix, "I am
more than four score years, whilst you are not fifty."
"That is true," answered Lavigerie, "but your Lordship
must remember that the circumstances are different.   We
count by miles as well as by years, and when the miles
are multiplied they also affect our nature.   So if you are
thirty years older than I, yet I have thousands of miles to
my account, and that reëstablishes the balance."   And
these thousands of miles he began early to travel.

He went from Larresorre to St. Nicholas' seminary, in Paris, where he spent the most gloomy period of his life. From the smiling landscape of Larresorre, with its limpid Nide, its majestic hills, and its extended horizon, to the black and gloomy seminary of St. Nicholas was too sudden a transition. His first months in Paris were truly a prison life; he longed for air and space, and he gave himself more to ennui than to study. Yet the students of St. Nicholas were amiable and jovial companions, and the superior, Father Dupanloup, that distinguished master who afterwards filled with such glory and honor the See of Orleans, was kind and considerate.

The little Basque was sad and morose; he longed for home and his native land, and buried in this gloom he promised to become a mediocre student. Father Dupanloup perceived the gifts of this child of nature; an energetic and an enthusiastic soul suddenly cast down by its exile from the paternal roof and the absence of the noonday sun, and he soon found a road to his pupil's heart. He led the young man safely through this enervating sentiment which paralyzes all efforts, and the pupil was worthy of the master. He learned the lesson; and after the death of the illustrious Bishop, he writes thus to Father Lagrange: "Amid the darkness, I saw another sun gradually arise which warmed my soul and awakened it from its deathly torpor. It was he who in the ardor of his spirits and in the warmth of that heart which was open to every noble sentiment, transported masters and pupils to the most lofty summits of the human and the divine. His manner, his walk, his expression, his lively faith—all combined to produce on us a blending of admiration, fear and respect. To those who knew him not, he might appear egotistic ; but to us he was the most humble of men. If he wished to have all, it was that he might give all to Jesus Christ, according to the divine plan of St. Paul : 'All things are for you, and you are for Christ.' "

Under such skilful direction, Charles Lavigerie became a brilliant student, for his quick intelligence and his love for study soon placed him at the head of his class, whilst his piety excited the admiration of everyone. The little boy of fourteen who had longed for a country parish, sprang into manhood, and preserved intact that grace of the sacerdotal vocation which he had confided to Bishop Lacroix. From St. Nicholas' seminary he went to Issey, where he spent one year in the study of philosophy, and in 1843, in the nineteenth year of his age, he entered the seminary of St. Sulpice.

CHAPTER II.

LAVIGERIE AT THE SEMINARY OF ST. SULPICE—AT THE SCHOOL OF CARMES—PRIEST AND PROFESSOR.

The masters of St. Sulpice, accustomed as they were to read the character of their students, soon discovered the qualities and the defects of young Lavigerie. At nineteen, he had not one perfection, but he had a character, and it was not difficult to foresee what hopes might be placed on that exceptional nature. He was, perhaps, a little stubborn and self-confident, but he had the defects of his qualities, and his qualities were of a superior order.

He had a correct judgment, a subtle and penetrating intellect, a lofty ideal which he would attain at any cost, a quickness of rejoinder which with one word refuted the arguments of his adversary, a tendency to sarcasm, which did not spare the feelings of a comrade, and which led him too often to sacrifice the perfection of fraternal charity for a witty saying; such were the qualities and the defects which at that period were most noticeable.

Withal, he was full of ardor, piety, love for study and confidence in God, which did not, however, exclude a certain amount of faith in human means. He believed in the direct intervention of Providence in the affairs of this world, but he also recognized the part which man must play. He was clear-sighted and just, he had settled principles, a talent for organization, and a direct manner which overawed his audience, and sometimes had the effect of offending the sensitive natures or of discouraging the timid. He knew not the hesitations and doubts which encumber mediocre intellects with the details and trivialities of a subject. In a word, he had a superior mind, but he was not easily understood; he won esteem, respect and admiration to a certain extent, for he had that force of character which warned men not to contend against his indisputable superiority.

At St. Sulpice as at St. Nicholas, the commencement appeared gloomy, but Mgr. Affre soon afforded an outlet for that secret struggle of an ardent soul amid the calm and monotonous year at the Seminary. Mgr. Affre was impressed with the progress and discoveries of modern science, and he saw the necessity of placing in the hands of the clergy those weapons with which they might counteract the false views of the enemies of the Church and of her eternal truths. He founded at Carmes, Paris, a superior normal school for the aspirants to the priesthood, and placed it under the direction of Father Cruice, afterwards Bishop of Marseilles. Lavigerie quitted St. Sulpice and repaired to Carmes to prepare for his degrees. He buried himself in his books, and in 1847 he received the Licentiate of Arts. As much to his honor and energy as to his obedience and intelligence, he who longed for active missionary life, silenced his desires and devoted himself to persevering study. He delved into the rich stores of Greek and Latin; he published a course of Greek exercise, Greek versions, a Greek and French dictionary, and an abridged history of the Church.

This literary discipline and victory over self softened the harsh angles of his character, and contributed not a little to that elegant facility of style which characterized his diocesan decrees, private letters and writings. This example is a powerful argument against the enemies of Latin and Greek; and it serves to demonstrate that these literary studies which are considered useless in this age of bankers, merchants, engineers and chemists, tend also to form men of action. When we are in touch with the lofty spirits whose language and thoughts are classic, the judgment is formed, the ideas are elevated, the intellect is refined, and that extended view, far from retarding the progress of the natural or the economic sciences, teaches how to place principle above comfort and material prosperity. Science becomes more amiable, enticing and accessible. The culture of the beautiful has an affinity with the culture of the good, for beautiful thoughts and beautiful language are not unfrequently the prelude of good acts.

After Lavigerie had received his degrees he returned to St. Sulpice, where he completed his course. The two years which he spent in this house ever remained a hallowed remembrance in his heart. Years afterward an old man, wearing a long white beard, the cross of a bishop on his breast, a cardinal's hat in his hand, entered the room of a seminarian of St. Sulpice. It was Cardinal Lavigerie. He humbly begged permission to say a prayer in that room, which he himself had formerly occupied, and the venerable Cardinal knelt at the foot of the bed and remained buried in recollection and prayer. He then led the seminarian to the window and told him that from that window he had witnessed the terrible days of the revolution of 1848. This anecdote evinces his sentiments for that sacred spot, which had sheltered his youth.

Lavigerie received Holy Orders at St. Sulpice July 2, 1849, but he was obliged to procure a dispensation on account of his age. Bishop Affre was not present to impose his hands upon the young priest, for he had fallen under the barricades of the revolution whilst in the act of imploring the grace of heaven for his people. Bishop Sibour gave to the Church this noble recruit, who would so actively and so generously serve her. One day he stood in that same sanctuary, a prince of the Church, and thanked God for the graces which he had received at his ordination. "I was then young," he said; "and now I am an old man! My youth! How everything in this church recalls it to me! I see before me again the students of my dear seminary where I spent so many

happy days. I see the altar at which I received Holy
Orders, the stones upon which I lay prostrate in proof of
my renunciation of this world. And yet with these sweet
remembrances are linked many painful thoughts. The
Archbishop of Paris, from whom I received subdeacon-
ship, was killed in the barricades; the Archbishop of
Paris, who raised me to the priesthood, was assassinated
in the sanctuary, and the Archbishop of Paris, whom I
replaced in my first episcopal see, was shot as a hostage—
great God! from what catastrophies have we not escaped!
And you, my dear children, weigh well what zeal, vigilance
and piety are necessary to render you worthy of your high
vocation."

Father Cruice, who highly esteemed Lavigerie, petitioned the Archbishop to appoint him professor of Latin
literature in the college of Carmes ; and whilst the young
priest brilliantly conducted his classes, he continued his
studies in preparation for his doctorate. The defence of
his thesis at the Sorbonne was a real triumph ; it treated
of Hegesippus, who is, after St. Luke, the most ancient
ecclesiastical historian. The French thesis bore the
modest title of "An Essay on the Christian Schools of
Edessa." The examiners were unanimous in their
decision, and Victor Leclerc, the dean of the faculty,
crowned the young laureate. The school of Carmes
had progressed rapidly in science and literature, but the
finances were so limited, that the Archbishop could not
conveniently support the professors ; so Father Lavigerie
accepted, besides his professorship, the post of chaplain to
two communities of nuns. He seemed to multiply the
hours as he so did during his entire life.

CHAPTER III.

FATHER LAVIGERIE, DOCTOR OF LETTERS AND PRO-FESSOR OF LITERATURE AT THE SORBONNE.

In 1764, towards the end of Louis XV's reign, a church was begun on the site of the old Abbey of St. Genevieve and dedicated to that saint, who is the patroness of Paris ; but the French Revolution prevented the completion of the work at that time. The Constituent Assembly took possession of St. Genevieve's and consecrated it to the memory of its patriots. The effect was felt on the architecture of the edifice. The original plan formed a cross, but the desecrators erected a dome in the centre and a columned portico in front, the pediment of which contained an immense bass-relief representing great men crowned by their country. The spectator could not know whether the edifice were a temple or a museum, a theatre or a church, and the insciption over the entrance, " By a grateful country to her great men," did not remove the doubt. The pagan name of pantheon was substituted for the Holy Shepherdess, and pious chants, hymns and ceremonies were prostituted to the coffins of military men, artists and writers. The crypt contained the tombs of the architect Soufflot, Rosseau, Voltaire, and many other Frenchmen of renown. Nothing disturbed the silence and sorrow of the tomb until the revolution of July, 1830, when the church . was restored to Catholic worship under the name of St. Genevieve.

The Archbishop who had long desired to fit ecclesiastics in an especial manner to preach the Word of God,
so that they might be abreast with the needs and difficulties of modern times, devoted the revenues of St.
Genevieve's church to the support of those who would
undertake this arduous mission.   The applicants were
obliged to pass a rigid examination before a board of
examiners who regulated their admission and rank.   The
success of Lavigerie attracted the attention of M. Maret,
the dean of the Sorbonne, who desired an assistant professor of ecclesiastical history.   He wrote to the Archbishop and to the Minister of Public Education the
following letter : "Father Lavigerie is one of the best
students of Carmes.   His scholarly essay on the school
of Edessa manifests a rare union of qualities which
betokens a good historian—aptitude and keenness of
appreciation, wise criticism, concise and agreeable style.
With care and study, he will become an excellent professor of church history.   Moreover, he has fixed principles in theology and philosophy."   This letter had the
desired effect, and Father Lavigerie was appointed to the
chair of ecclesiastical history at the Sorbonne.

The Sorbonne, which is the seat of the University of
Paris, was founded in 1250 by Robert of Sorbonne, the
chaplain of St. Louis ; and it was intended especially for
students of theology.   In the seventeenth century, the
architect, Jacques Lemercier, enlarged the school and the
church, but what is now called under the collective name
of the university, was the creation of Napoleon I, who
grouped the faculties of archæology, history, moral and
political sciences, and geography under the management

of the Minister of Public Instruction. The old Sorbonne had no architectural beauty, hence a reconstruction of the buildings was begun in 1884, under the direction of Nenot, but the old church which contained the tomb of Richelieu was retained on account of its artistic merit.

Father Lavigerie enhanced the literary and the theological reputation of the school, and he attracted general attention by the subject of his first year—the Jansenist and the Gallican errors. These two errors were not dead in France, anything sufficed to call forth a harsh polemic or rouse the anger of the last supporters of a sect which strove to gain recruits. The Jansenists had at their service the *Catholic Observer*, a journal edited and directed by Guettee, an apostate priest, who culminated his religious evolutions by becoming a Russian Pope. This journal, which was Catholic only in name, took offence at the subject which Father Lavigerie had selected. " We have never," it remarked, " been present at Father Lavigerie's lectures. Not that we would not appreciate them, but we dislike public discourses, because much time is lost for a small return. However, we shall follow the lectures of the professor of ecclesiastical history on account of the subject which he has chosen."

This opposition did not disconcert the young priest, but his avowed Roman tendencies irritated the supporters of the *Observer*. " How is it possible," they maintained, "that the entire Sorbonne can adhere to a young priest who was unknown yesterday, and who wishes to demolish the old Gallican traditions to rear on the smoking ruins the undefined dogma of the Papal Infallibility?" We must remember that this was in 1854, sixteen years before the definition of that dogma which the Jansenists called a novelty. There was open warfare against the audacious professor. The *Observer* established a crusade against the course of lectures, and loudly abused him, but this hostiiity only added to his popularity. The Jansenistic paper supplicated the Archbishop to dismiss him. "If," said they, "he were only a professorof the University, we would not find fault with the enunciation of his belief; but he is a priest, and he receives his mission to teach from the Archbishop of Paris, and his mission allows him to teach only Catholic truth. Therefore we are obliged to denounce his heretical and rationalistic teachings to the Archbishop of Paris, who is the custodian of the truth in his own diocese, and who cannot authorize such pernicious doctrines. Father Lavigerie has replaced the old dogmas of the Church by several new ones, and amongst others, the 'Infallibility of the Pope.'" The Archbishop's reply was prompt and expressive : "Father Lavigerie has been appointed professor for this year, and he has already selected his course of lectures."

By a series of circumstances, which Father Lavigerie had neither courted nor desired, his active and practical spirit was absorbed by speculative truths. God in His all-wise designs had led him through the various grades of the ministry to mature by the weight of experience that judgment which would exert such an influence in the foundation of educational establishments. He began his work amongst the young as president of the Ozanam Conference, known to-day as the Catholic Circle of Luxemburg Street. Amongst those ardent and ambitious spirits he experienced some emotions of that missionary zeal which burned in his heart from his infancy. In his chair at the Sorbonne he reached the mind and the intelligence of his audience; in the Catholic Circle he dealt with their souls.

Father Perreyne, who succeeded him as professor of history, once remarked that a man was not elevated to the priesthood simply to deliver a course of lectures or to write a beautiful article now and then for the magazines. The future Archbishop of Algiers proposed the same question to himself. He thirsted for active life and for noble works, and his soul was stifled in the confinement of the university; but this was only his hour of trial and preparation, and God was providentially preparing a work which would hurry him for the remainder of his life into the heat of the battle.

CHAPTER IV.

FATHER LAVIGERIE DIRECTOR OF THE SOCIETY FOR THE PROMOTION OF EDUCATION IN THE EAST.

In 1830, during the reign of Charles X., the Dey of Algiers insulted France in the person of her consul, and a French squadron was sent to Algiers. War was declared, and after a vigorous struggle the French gained partial possession of the country, but the victory of Charles X. remained for fifteen years a disputed question. A deep instinctive hatred arose between the Mussulmans and the Christians. The Arabs yielded to force, but they were neither conquered nor convinced, and the chiefs and the nomadic tribes endeavored at every opportunity to shake off their hated yoke.

Amongst the most obstinate and persistent against Christian civilization was the Emir Abd-el-Kader. This man stands out as a grand and noble character. At the age of twenty, he wielded so much power and influence that the Dey of Algiers, jealous of his ascendancy over his compatriots, endeavored to destroy him. The overthrow of the government of the Dey increased the popularity of the Emir, and made him a formidable enemy of the French. He persistently besieged the strong cities, and France was forced to render an account to this adversary whose alliance was most necessary to her success. He ruled over the province of Mascara, but this semblance of royalty did not satisfy his ambitions and aspirations, for he desired the complete and absolute independence of his country. He struggled twelve years to realize this dream of his life, but he was forced in 1847 to surrender to General Lamoricier with the promise of complete liberty. France feared to keep her word, and Abd-el-Kader, crushed by the law of might, was led a captive to the castle of Amboise, in France. This want of faith deeply wounded the savage son of the desert, yet the mild treatment of his custodians made on him a lasting impression. His upright and generous nature learned to love France. Napoleon III., guided by a rare inspiration, opened the gates of his prison and restored his liberty. This confidence was not misplaced ; for he remained until death a faithful ally to France, and in his retirement at Damascus he soon found occasion to manifest by his actions and sympathy that sincere friendship.

French influence in the East goes back to the Crusades, but when Abd-el-Kader retired to Damascus this influence was waning; for there, as in Africa, the servants of Christ and the followers of Mahomet were in constant warfare. The Mussulman abhorred the name of Christian; his only argument of proselytism was the sword, and he incessantly harrassed the French Christian settlements. Notwithstanding these perils, devout and courageous souls did not hesitate to risk their lives in the cause of religion. Syria was flooded each year by missioners, religious, and Sisters of Charity, and the civilization of the people was begun in the Christian schools. A society was formed whose object was the extension of the political and the religious influence of France in the East by means of education. The committee assembled at Paris in the beginning of 1856, at the residence of Baron Cauchy, a member of the Academy of Sciences. Although it was an assembly of illustrious names such as Montalembert, De Broglie and Ozanam, men who were ever in readiness when their religion or their country appealed to their devotion, yet little progress was made, for money was required without which the work could not be continued. M. Vallon, the secretary to the association, made his report after a year of struggle and failure; he had collected only three thousand dollars, which was not sufficient to meet the demands.

Prince Gazarin, a converted Russian, who had become a Jesuit with the hope of bringing back to the true fold his brethren of the Eastern church, felt intense grief at this failure. An eloquent and influential man who would thoroughly organize the work and gain the interest of the people was necessary. Father Lavigerie, the doctor of the Sorbonne was the man. Full of this idea, Father

Gazarin acquainted the confessor of Lavigerie with this proposition. Father Lavigerie himself relates this evolution from his life as a professor. "My confessor," he says, "was the saintly and renowned Father Ravignan, whose memory I hold in the most tender reverence. I was drawn to him by his virtue, his lofty character and by the remembrance of a common country, for he was from Bayonne, where I spent my childhood days, almost under the shadow of the old cathedral. This great man, who was an experienced master in the conduct of souls, never directly condemned my life of study and of teaching, but he would casually remark that he saw another life for me. One day he told me that Father Gazarin had explained to him the difficulty which the society had encountered. They had resolved to entrust the management of affairs to a reliable ecclesiastic. And then he said to me with a smile, 'These men of the institute have naturally turned to you, and they have requested me to inform you of their decision.' I was neither surprised nor disturbed at such an avowal. 'If you think,' I replied, 'that such is God's will, I am prepared.' 'It is God's will,' he answered; and with these words the affair was concluded."

"And whither have they led me for thirty years? To France, Asia, Rome and Africa, and now this long voyage draws to a happy close, and brings me safely into port again. On the next day, Father Gazarin conducted me to my small apartment on the second floor of a house on Regard street, where the office of the society has since been established. He led me as a conqueror might lead his captive, but I was a willing captive. On the way I received the congratulation of Admiral Mathieu, who shortly afterwards entrusted to me the registers and the scant fund, which was easily managed. This was at the close of the year 1856. Father Gazarin remarked as he departed from the office: 'You see the water, my dear Father, now you must swim.'"

The first requirement in replenishing an empty treasury, is to become a beggar, and the unanimous verdict is that the life of the beggar is not a sinecure. Begging was the life work of Father Lavigerie, for as bishop and prince of the Church his hand was outstretched to the world. We may add that, although French generosity is inexhaustible, especially when a great man intercedes for a worthy undertaking, the impressions of Father Lavigerie as a mendicant friar were not always pleasant. He preserved the remembrances of his adventures, and often in his conversation he would recur to this period of his life. One day, whilst presenting to the priests of his diocese the missionary bishop of Picando, he remarked, with emotion: "Ask the blessing of Bishop Livinhac for you and for me. Remember the trials which he has undergone for Jesus Christ and the chains of martyrdom which have bound his hands." And then a smile banished the tears of pity, and he added: "With these hands what rich bequests might not I obtain for my mission!" Yet he needed not the hands of his neighbor, for he knew how to extend his own with an indefatigable perseverance for the promotion of the schools of the East.

The diocese of Paris was under the care of the saintly Cardinal Marlot, the successor of Mgr. Tibour, who had fallen under the dagger of an assassin in the Church of

St. Stephen of the Mount.   Lavigerie obtained the blessing of the Archbishop and started on his journey.   He
preached first in Paris, then in the neighboring cities—
Versailles, Chartres, Caen, Orleans, Angers and Nantes.
After a brief vacation he went to the south of France.
This journey was not all pleasure, for after the sermon he
made his quest; then he formed a committee, appointed
a director and organized a local centre.   The hearty
encouragement of the bishops and his own fiery eloquence
bore abundant fruit.   Yet, amid the roses, he often found
thorns which deeply wounded his zeal.   "I have sometimes," he said, "been refused in terms which were flattering neither to my reason nor to my person.   Some people
knew not of the schools of the East, nor of the Sorbonne,
nor of Father Lavigerie.   If I insisted, they informed me
that I was a swindler who had appeared recently in the
neighboring cities under a religious garb, and that the
police were in search of me."

At other times the authorities were influenced by personal motives in placing obstacles in his path.   The bishop
of a certain city was erecting a cathedral.   When he heard
that Father Lavigerie proposed to preach in his diocese he
was fearful, and not without cause, that the resources which
he much needed would be appropriated to the cause of
'religion in the East.   He departed from the city, but only
after he had amply instructed his Vicar-General to dis-
courage the mendicant friar.

The Vicar-General played his part well—he was both
politic and polite.   He heartily approved of Lavigerie's
mission, but he added: "I see that you do not clearly
grasp the situation.   Our people take no interest in foreign

works, for more than four supplicants have failed during
the past weeks. You will not have one person at your
sermon." The stern perseverance of Lavigerie could
not admit a defeat. "Ah, well," he replied, "nothing
risked, nothing gained. I am accustomed to small audi-
ences, for at the Sorbonne I had only twenty-five students.
I am of the school of St. Francis—one soul is sufficient.
If three persons are present I will be satisfied."

He preached to a large audience, and as he was not
allowed to ask for assistance in the church, he requested
all who were interested in the work to accompany him to
the sacristy. They arose as one man, and contributed a
sum which allowed over five hundred dollars for the Eastern schools.

Lavigerie was delighted, and he resolved to make a
visit from house to house, although the Vicar-General did
all in his power to prevent him. "Do not petition the
people," he said, "you will have all the hardship without
any reward. Failure is certain, as you shall see." "Well,"
replied the Father, "I shall see." "No," added the Vicar-
General, "we shall see, for I shall be pleased to accompany you"; and he followed Lavigere step by step, and
everywhere he introduced him very politely: "I have
the honor of introduucing to you one of the most distinguished professors of the Sorbonne, Father Lavigerie,
who is now the director of the work for the promotion
of education in the East. He is endeavoring to interest
the Catholics in this undertaking, but as the bishop
has justly remarked, it is impossible to establish a
new work here, for we are overburdened with our
own works." At the third visit Father Lavigerie inter-

rupted his guide; " I see," said he, " that the Vicar-General calumniates the bishop and yourselves, but I do not
believe him, for I know how eager you have always been
to do good." This reply silenced his opponent. The
pastor of one of the churches invited him to deliver a
lecture, and this time the Vicar-General was thoroughly
aroused. " No," he said, " the bishop does not allow it."
Father Lavigerie gently remarked that the bishop did not
even know of the pastor's invitation. " No matter,"
angrily replied the Vicar-General, " if he did know he
would not give his permission." Father Lavigerie
heartily enjoyed this incident, and ever afterwards he told
it with much zest.

"At another time," he writes, " I received a more severe
repulse. The pastor of a cathedral closed the door in my
face. But I had the opportunity of gaining a singular
revenge, for some years afterwards, on the death of the
bishop, I was offered the vacant see. I smiled when I
thought of the sorry figure of the young priest who
would be obliged to admit with all due solemnity the man
whom he had so rudely rejected. But I was appointed
over the Diocese of Nancy, and I lost the opportunity of
recalling to his mind that ' the King of France does not
revenge the insults of the Duke of Orleans.' "

CHAPTER V.

FATHER LAVIGERIE IN THE EAST—AUDITOR
OF THE ROTA.

Towards the close of 1859, the old hatred of the
Mahometan Druises towards the Christian Maronites

broke out anew; and some fanatics recruited hordes of brigands anxious for any crime or violence. Abd-el-Kader, although a Mahometan and an inhabitant of Damascus, was not taken into their counsel, nor could he understand the motive of the leaders. Suddenly, throughout all Syria the signal for massacre was given. In the towns and villages, but especially in the districts in which the French were unable to protect the population against this frenzy, frightful crimes were committed. Conflagration, pillage, assassination, every means was employed for the extermination of the poor Christians.

The Mahometan government silently acquiesced in this violence; and the Sultan was almost powerless, placed as he was between his fanatic co-religionists and the fear of France which exercised the right of protection over the Christians of Egypt. Five thousand towns and villages were razed to the ground, sixty thousand Christians assassinated, and sixty thousand starved wretches were left to wander aimlessly amid the smoking ruins. Such was the sad spectacle which in three months Syria presented to Europe. The newspapers and the dispatches of the consuls had imparted the sad news to the civilized world, but their descriptions were only general and mitigated sketches of scenes which would strike terror into the most valiant heart. The Druises manifested a refinement of cruelty in excess of the most bloody wars, for Syria was not a field of battle but of carnage. The Christians fled to the mountains only to be tortured by the horrors of famine.

The Mussulmans massacred husbands and wives, mothers with children in their arms, the aged and the sick ; none escaped that excess of barbarity, the very recital of which makes one shudder. Close by the palace of Dier-el-Kamar stands a wall in which there is an opening about the height of a man. They confined their victims in this enclosure, and obliged them to pass their arms through the opening ; then they amused themselves by giving a reward to the soldier who would most adroitly cut off the wrists. These atrocities lasted three months, hence we may imagine the despair and exasperation of the poor Maronites. The vultures, which fed on the sad remains, were 'unable completely to devour the traces of the victims.

Sometimes despair drove the poor Christians to seek revenge. One day a Christian woman saw on the streets of Dier-el-Kamar the wife of her husband's murderer. Infuriated with anger, she seized a sword, and signing herself with the sign of the Cross, she rushed upon the woman, and before the authorities could interfere, she with one blow cut off her head. At the first news of the insurrection, France dispatched troops to Syria under the command of General Beaufort d'Hautpoul. When the Sultan learned of their arrival, he sought out some guilty Druises and punished them; thus he hoped to appease the indignation of the French, and prevent them from penetrating into the interior of the country. He did not wish them to scrutinize too closely the extent and the enormity of the disasters. But General d'Hautpoul concluded that the repression had not been effectual, and he advanced to the interior. Yet, if this small army held some brigands in subjection, it could never repair the evil, alleviate the miseries, nor console the poor Christians who had outlived such a disaster.

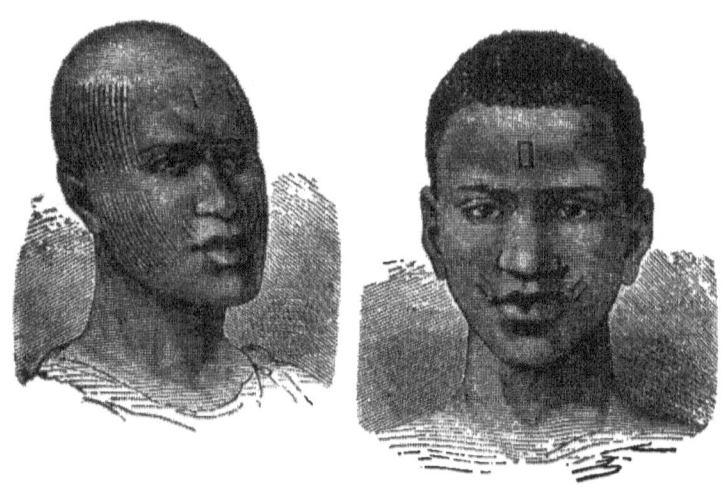

FROM THE SOUTHERN SOUDAN.

This role was reserved for Father Lavigerie. He appealed to the French clergy ; again he stretched forth his hand for aid. "Thousands of Christians," he said, "pitilessly massacred by the fanatic hordes, women out-raged, priests and religious tortured and abandoned with-out burial ; everywhere pillage, incendiary and violence ; such is the sad news each day from Syria. The fugitive Maronites, driven from their homes, have for the past two months lived in the mountains, tortured by the pangs of hunger and the fear of the sword which a barbarian chief has sworn he will not return to the scabbard until he has beheaded the last man who makes the sign of the Cross. Many women and children have sought refuge from dis-honor or death in the homes of our sisters and priests. These poor creatures appeal to France ; to her the groans of the martyrs and the confessors of our faith arise. But how shall we repair the evils ? The Society for the Pro-motion of Education in the East raises its voice, persuaded that the Catholics of France have not forgotten the ancient ties which bind them to the Maronite nation, so justly called 'the France of the East.' In all confidence I call on you ; I beg the aid of your zeal for this work of charity and faith."

This eloquent appeal was heard throughout France, and gifts and alms flooded the small apartment on Regard street. The heart of the French is ever open to charity ; almost a million dollars in money and supplies were donated. Such a remembrance of kindness will keep the most pessimistic from despairing of a nation which, not-withstanding its peculiarities and revolts, belongs to Him who suffers not the glass of water given in His name to go unrewarded.

Father Lavigerie undertook the distribution of the alms. He little cared for the displeasure of his pupils at the University, for he preferred to make history rather than to recount it. After a hurried preparation he set out for the East, and what he there beheld confirmed forever his missionary vocation. Bishop Lacroix was a true prophet, for God had conducted the little Charles afar off, much farther than he himself had anticipated. For six months he wandered amid the ruins caused by the fierce Mussulmans, and everywhere he gave alms and consolation to the poor Maronites, who lavished praises and blessings on France and the French people. This dangerous journey he accomplished with his faithful dragoman, Michael Rose. He visited successively the Christian villages which had been spared, and the villages which had been abandoned to pillage. The Maronite Bishops, the United Greeks, the Armenians and Syrians regarded him as a messenger sent by God. With his natural tact and his knowledge of the needs of the situation, he established in the East lasting institutions. He found at Beirut an orphanage for four hundred Maronite girls, and a similar establishment for boys at Zahleh. He distributed the French money equally throughout Syria, saddened only by the thought that the poor Syrians, who were equally destitute, could lay no claim to these alms.

He resolved to visit the survivors of Deir-el-Kadar, that he might revive their courage and fill them with the hope of better days by offering up the sacrifice of the Mass in their ruined church. The French consul assisted officially at the sacrifice, and the military commander placed a guard at the disposal of Father

Lavigerie. Amid the intense silence, broken only by the tears and the sighs of the congregation, the officer at the moment of the Consecration, gave the command: "Fall on your knees," followed by the roll of the drum, which shook the building. On his way to Hamah, he was violently thrown from his horse, and suffered a broken arm and a dislocated shoulder. The poor inhabitants were disconsolate. "We are destined," they cried, "to misfortune. Our village will be accursed in the eyes of our benefactor, for he will no longer wish good to Hamah." They little knew the messenger whom God had sent them. "The most pleasant remembrance of that expedition," writes he, "was the poor people of the mountain."

As soon as he was able to sit in the saddle, he departed for Damascus. More than eight thousand persons had perished in the Christian quarters which had been pillaged for twenty-two days. Only one Mussulman attempted to stay the evil, but he was overpowered by the number and the ferocity of his co-religionists, and yet he contrived to save some Christians. This courageous and noble man was the former prisoner of the Amboise castle, Abd-el-Kader. Lavigerie desired to pay his respects to the chief, and to present to him the compliments of Bishop Dupech of Algiers. "Tell him," said the Bishop, "that his noble conduct towards the Christians has not surprised me, for I have never known a man who practiced natural justice better than he." Abd-el-Kader received this high eulogy with becoming modesty. "I have only done my duty," he replied, "yet I am pleased to know that France appreciates my conduct. I love France, and I shall never forget what I have received from her."

The knowledge of Father Lavigerie's good deeds had preceded him to his native land, and on his return the Minister of Religion supplicated the Emperor to confer on him the Cross of the Legion of Honor. The Oriental bishops sent to Pope Pius IX a testimonial of their esteem and admiration for him who had so generously aided them in their hour of distress. The attention of the Pope was thus drawn to the young professor of the Sorbonne. Bishop Tour-d'Auvergne, the Auditor of the Rota from France, had been appointed Coadjutor-Bishop of Bourges, and Father Lavigerie was named for this important position, which had been recently established by the Emperor, Napoleon III. He entered into his new functions in October, 1860. Every Monday and Friday the tribunal of the Rota assembled at the Vatican to investigate all the spiritual affairs of the Catholic world—questions of immunities, marriages, rites, benefices and the canonization of saints. Yet this honorable post, by no means a sinecure, did not satisfy the activity of the new prelate. He accepted the position only on condition that he should retain the dictatorship of the Eastern schools and be permitted to establish in Rome a council similar to the council of Paris. He then departed for Italy, leaving as his successor the worthy and talented Father Perreyve.

CHAPTER VI.

FATHER LAVIGERIE IS CONSECRATED BISHOP OF NANCY—HIS BRIEF SOJOURN IN LORRAINE.

The Auditor of the Rota seldom remains long in Rome, for this position is usually the stepping-stone to the Episcopacy. In the opinion of the French government, the activity and the energy of Father Lavigerie adapted him for diocesan work. So, on March 5, 1863, he was appointed over the diocese of Nancy, and his consecration was fixed for the 25th, at the national church of St. Louis of the French. Pius IX, who highly esteemed him, would have presided had he not been prevented by a severe attack of illness. He delegated Cardinal Villecourt, who was assisted by Bishops Hohenlohe and Marrinelli.

The consecrating prelate and the newly-consecrated prelate presented the most perfect contrast. They were both French, both destined to wear the purple, both warmly attached to the Holy See, yet they possessed different gifts and merits which were universally recognized. Apart from the feelings of piety and faith with which Bishop Lavigerie regarded the solemnities of the Church, and the more intimate and personal feast-days of his sacerdotal career, he delighted in pomp and display. He invited to his consecration the Prince of Tour-d'Aubergne, the attachés of the French Embassy and of the Tribunal of the Rota. He was pleased to be the hero of a religious and a French celebration, and he desired to give to the ceremony that eclat with which all his life he surrounded himself whenever he had an opportunity of displaying a patriotic or a religious sentiment.

Cardinal Villecourt was of a different disposition, for he was rather a religious than a prince of the Church. As Bishop Lavigerie appeared great, and desired to perform great actions for the glory of God and for the honor of the Church, so the Cardinal desired to conceal himself through a sentiment of humility and voluntary abasement, and in perfect imitation of his Master, who was born in a stable, and who died on a cross.   These contrasts in the Shepherds of God's flock illustrate the extent of that religion which draws from various characters and disposi- tions varied and real good.   The old styled coach of Car- dinal Villecourt, his stained throne and his threadbare furniture might excite a smile, but His Holiness com- manded the respect of all.

It is said that when Pius IX informed him of his eleva- tion to the Cardinalate, he was so disturbed that for eight days he could neither eat nor sleep.   He could not make known his grief, for the Pope had not officially elevated him ; but his servant observed his chagrin, and he loudly commented on it: " Monseigneur is sad, and he does not wish to tell me the cause."   " What do you wish, my poor John ? " said the Cardinal, " something most unex- pected and extraordinary has happened to me."   " Do not be disturbed," added John," " even if you go to the end of the world, I will follow you."   The poor Bishop could no longer keep his secret from his devoted servant. "Ah, well," he said, " I may tell you my sorrow ; I am a Cardinal ! "   John knew not whether to laugh or to cry, but when he saw new servants in the palace, and he, him- self, the major-domo of a great house, he took more agreeably than his master to the idea of a Cardinal, and he rebuked his master for his vexation at so high a position.

Bishop Lavigerie was full of life and activity.   To rule a diocese, in which faith and piety were in demand, was not displeasing to him.   He saw a vast field of labor, and no sooner was he consecrated, than he courageously set about his work. His first pastoral letter, written from Rome, indicates his desire of toiling for the love of God, and of arising above miserable party quarrels. "I should bring, and I do bring into your midst," he said, "one standard—the standard of Jesus Christ and His Church. With the help of God I shall ever be a stranger to dissentions or personal interest. Placed outside and above the world, I wish only one thing—the salvation of your souls, for I love you all, no matter from what clime you may come."

With that accurate foresight and penetration which enabled him to perceive dangers in advance, he began by an administrative act which to-day clearly proves his clear-headedness. He saw the importance of Christian schools. The young are the future of a country, and is not that future in the hands of their instructors? The diocese of Nancy which was eminently Catholic, counted a considerable number of religious at the head of the schools and educational establishments; but privileges had been accorded them against which the public spirit secretly protested. They were admitted as teachers without having passed an examination of competency. For the majority this confidence was justifiable, but it gave rise to criticism and malevolent insinuations against the lack of education in some of the teachers. The Bishop of Nancy, forestalling the Minister of Public Instruction, issued an ordinance which was severely condemned by all the teaching communities of the diocese. He required all the novices to pass an examination before an episcopal board, composed of the best instructed ecclesiastics. After a successful examination they obtained a diploma, without which they could not teach the lowest grades of a school. Were this measure universal the ostracism which to-day brands our Christian schools might be averted. In the first moments of astonishment the religious raised many objections, but they were true to their duty of obedience, and as the Bishop had anticipated, the trial turned to their honor.

Some of his confreres thought he had made a humilating concession to the spirit of the age. They complained to the Nuncio at Paris, who officially informed him that the Pope was dissatisfied with his action, and had ordered him immediately to withdraw his ordinance. He did not hesitate in his submission to the Holy See, but he felt that he was in the right, and he desired to justify himself. He set out for Rome without acquainting anyone of his journey, and skillfully avoiding the tardiness and delays of etiquette, he requested an audience with His Holiness on an affair of importance. Pius IX, who dearly loved the former Auditor of the Rota, gave him a private audience, but not without much astonishment at his precipitate journey. He immediately asked the object of his request. "Most Holy Father, it is the command which you sent me to withdraw my ordinance." "What ordinance," asked the Pope, "I have commanded you to withdraw an ordinance?" Bishop Lavigerie then explained the affair, and he was informed that the Nuncio had acted on his own responsibility. He requested an examination of the ordinance by the Congregation of Bishops and Regulars. The result was an absolute approbation of the measure, with the express desire that it be introduced into the other dioceses. With this approbation, the Bishop hastened to the Nuncio, who reiterated his orders. In reply, Bishop Lavigerie drew from his pocket the decision of Rome, and quitted the palace before that official representative had recovered from his surprise. ,

---

CHAPTER VII.

LAVIGERIE IS MADE ARCHBISHOP OF ALGIERS.

One year after the elevation of Bishop Lavigerie to the See of Nancy, Marshal MacMahon was appointed Governor-General of Algeria. Marie Edme Patrick Maurice MacMahon was born at the chateau of Sully, near Autun, June 13th, 1808. He was descended from an Irish family which took refuge in France after the fall of the Stuarts. He entered the military school of St. Cyr in 1825, and began active service in the expedition into Algeria. He was made Brigadier-General in 1848, and assumed command of a division in the Crimean war. In 1857, he fought in Algeria against the Kabyles, and was appointed Commander-in-Chief of the land and sea forces in Africa. He was recalled for the Compaign against Austria, and on account of his victory at Magenta, he received from Napoleon on the field of battle the dignity of Marshal of France and the title Duke of Magenta. He was fitted by his knowledge of Africa for the post of Governor-General of Algeria which had been lately subdued by France.

Unfortunately a man may be a hero on the field of battle and yet be only a mediocre administrator. In this

respect MacMahon often surprised those who rejoiced at
his promotion. They thought that a man who was a
good Christian, a worthy citizen, and an upright and
intrepid soldier, should also possess exceptional administrative qualifications. The Governor of Algeria is
almost the sovereign of the country, for his distance from
the mother country enables him to regulate affairs
beyond appeal. But he has the responsibilities as well as
the privileges of royalty, and since the conquest, the
kingdom of Africa was not a pacific royalty. From the
time of Abd-el-Kader, insurrections were so numerous
that a military government was imposed on the Arabs.
But a moral and a religious influence was also necessary
to transform these Mussulman into loyal subjects of
France.

Two Catholic Archbishops had presided over the See of
Algiers. The first, Archbishop Dupech, whose courage
and devotions were untiring, was overwhelmed with difficulties. On his arrival in the colony in 1838, he had
three priests and no permanent institutions; but one year
afterwards he counted twenty-five priests, eight churches,
seven chapel, one seminary, eight Catholic schools, two
orphanages and one hospital. His zeal burdened him
with debts, and consequently, in the eyes of his enemies,
he had compromised the episcopal dignity. After an
administration of ten years, he quitted Algeria; but not
before he had reaped a harvest sufficiently abundant to
merit the pardon of posterity for his supposed sin of
extravagance. Thanks to the generosity of Napoleon III.,
the first Archbishop died neither insolvent nor a prisoner
for his debts.

And now the Governor-General was occupied with the thought of a successor to Archbishop Pavy, who had just died. Two days later he dispatched the following letter to the Bishop of Nancy:

"COMPEIGNE, November 17, 1866.

"Monseigneur :—I have been informed of the death of Arch-bishop Pavy, and I desire to present the name of his successor whenever his Majesty shall see fit to consult me. After mature reflection, I can propose no more worthy candidate, nor one better fitted for the Archdiocese of Algeria, than the present Bishop of Nancy. This is my firm conviction, yet I cannot act until I know your feelings. I beg you to inform me whether you will accept the position. It is one of the most important that could be confided to a clergyman of France. The difficulties are numerous, but I am persuaded that this thought will not arrest a man of your character and zeal.

"Hoping to hear from you at your earliest convenience,
"I remain, yours in Christ,
"MARSHAL MACMAHON."

Bishop Lavigerie was willing and prepared for the sacrifice. He was the superior of the most Catholic diocese of France, but in his ardor and zeal he felt that he had not watered it enough with his labor and sweat. Algiers was a poor diocese, composed mostly of Mussulmans, who scorned the Gospel and who warred against the Cross. At Nancy, everything was peace and happiness; at Algiers, all was turmoil, but he did not hesitate in his reply. "After mature reflection and prayer," he writes, "that God might direct my reply to your Excellency, I will clearly state my mind. I have never desired to quit this diocese, to which I am sincerely attached, and in which I have begun numerous works. Had your Excellency proposed a See of more importance than Nancy, I would have declined your offer, for I have entered the episcopacy through a motive of devotedness and sacrifice. You offer me a hard and laborious mission, one that involves exile and abandonment of all that is dear to me. You think that I am best adapted for the position. A Catholic Bishop can make only one reply; I accept the sacrifice, and if the Emperor appeal to my devotion, I shall not hesitate, cost what it may. I freely authorize your Excellency to make known my reply to his Majesty."

Bishop Lavigerie became the third Archbishop of the See of Algiers, which boasts of such illustrious names as Cyprian, Augustine and Fulgentius; and as they in former times, so he now must contend against innumerable obstacles. The Archdiocese of Algiers contained eighty-three parishes; four hundred regular and secular priests; four religious communities—the Lazarists, the Trappists, the Jesuits, and the Christian Brothers; six communities of women—the Sisters of St. Vincent de Paul, of the Sacred Heart, of the Christian Doctrine, of the Good Shepherds, of the Trinity of Valence, and of the Bon Secour of Troyes; and one large and one preparatory seminary. These zealous congregations labored amongst the Christians of the parishes and amongst the eight thousand who were scattered here and there in the French colony. They lived in the midst of Mussulmans, whom the mother country carefully guarded from any attempt of proselytism. This has been the great mistake of the French government in Africa, and Marshal MacMahon, although an exemplary Christian, shared in these false views. The politicians proposed to convert Africa into a French province by governing with a rod of iron, yet under a specious pretext of respect for the liberty of the Arabs, they decried any effort to introduce Christianity.

Doubtless, Marshal MacMahon did not think that he would have to deal with so stubborn an adversary when he selected Bishop Lavigerie for the See of Algiers, but this choice, which was the beginning of a prolonged struggle, was a manifest indication of the designs of Providence over the African colony. With an evangelical liberty which was, at the same time, firm and respectful, Archbishop Lavigerie fulfilled his duty and maintained his rights against every opponent. Thus he evinced his patriotism, for patriotism was the dominant virtue of this man, who was endowed with a political genius which our age has often misconstrued. It was patriotism and zeal for the salvation of souls which determined him to exchange his flourishing diocese for an impoverished one, a determination which astonished the entire French Hierarchy. We live in an age in which the supernatural and the patriotic virtues merit little consideration. Hence a majority of the bishops could not conceal their surprise at the conduct of Archbishop Lavigerie, and some even felt obliged to intercede with his friends to prevent his departure. But his action seemed to him only a better means of serving the sacred cause of the Church and of France.

He did not think with Marshal MacMahon that an Arabian and Mussulman kingdom could subsist under a French and Catholic yoke. He saw beyond this. To him the final conquest of Africa, of which Algiers was the key, consisted in complete assimilation. Instead of maintaining the false principle that a Mussulman is incapable of accepting the truths of Christianity, it was necessary to

attempt his conversion.   This difficult task did not deter
the Archbishop.   Two things seemed necessary—works
of charity for all, and French schools for the children.
He did not look forward to a complete realization of this
plan during his life, but he wished to give to it his encouragement and his labor.   Certainly, a tranquil and an hon-
ored life in France was more agreeable, but he sought
neither tranquility nor honor.   He was young, strong and
energetic, and he feared not the hardships of Algerian
life.   Only one man gave him any encouragement—Bishop
Maret, the former dean of the Sorbonne.   " Go," he said
to him, " God has chosen you.   I know the French hierarchy, and I know that you alone can attempt this work
with some chance of success," and Pius IX. was of the
same opinion.

On March 27, 1867, Bishop Lavigerie was consecrated
Archbishop of Algiers, and on December 22d he embarked
from Marseilles for his new field of labor.   The vessel on
which he took passage, although one of the smallest of the
line, carried over seven hundred passengers and a large
cargo of merchandise.   The Archbishop was accompanied
by a number of ecclesiastics, the superior of the Trappists,
several religious of the Sacred Heart and of other communities.   The captain had hardly steered across the Gulf
of Lyons when a heavy storm arose, and the vessel was
tossed from wave to wave.   In vain the sailors labored to
bring her to shore; the high sea broke the tiller, the
waters reached the hold and extinguished the fires of the
engines.   The Archbishop could only exhort the terrified
passengers to resignation and sorrow for their sins.   He
gave them a general absolution and requested them to

make a vow to "Our Lady of Africa" for their safety.
He then descended to the cabin, where he met the superior
of the Trappists. "Ah, dear Father Abbot," he said, "we
have just made a vow to 'Our Lady of Africa.' All here
will see that the Blessed Virgin will deliver us from this
peril; and you, what are you doing here?" "I also,"
replied the Trappist, "am recommending myself to our
good Mother. I am telling 'Our Lady of Africa,' in all
simplicity, that this disaster is not to her credit, for everyone knows that you and the priests and the religious are
invoking her aid. Now, if she allows us to perish, no one
will ever place confidence in her new shrine." The prelate smiled at this filial familiarity, but he himself had
made a vow from the depth of his heart to the good Virgin for these poor mariners. As Bishop Belzunce of
Marseilles had chosen "Our Lady of Trust" as the Protectress of seafaring people, so "Our Lady of Africa"
had become on the other side of the Mediterranean a place
of pilgrimage and of prayer for the poor sailors.

Six days after this storm, the ship and her cargo entered
the harbor of Algiers. And now as the visitor on a
Sunday afternoon wanders into the basilica which over-
looks the Arabian city, a strange sight meets his view.
Under the portico is a cenotaph erected by the Archbishop
of Algiers, on which is the following inscription: "To
the memory of those who have perished in the sea, and
who have been engulfed by the waves." A priest, vested
in a black cope and accompanied by four choir boys, goes
to the brow of the hill against which the waves lash. As
on All Souls' day, he intones the "Libera me, Domine."
The choir boys hold a pall over the abyss of waters, and

incense and holy water are cast to the East, and the West and the North in benediction of those who repose in this immense tomb.   This is the vow of Archbishop Lavigerie and of the passengers who were safely guided into port by the affectionate hand of Mary.

CHAPTER VIII.

ARCHBISHOP LAVIGERIE AND THE FAMINE OF 1867.

Two scourges treacherously lie in wait for the African people, the drought and the locust.   Two years of a drought and an invasion of the locusts reduced this unfortunate country to all the horrors of famine.   The poor starved to death, and the streets and the fields were filled with corpses, which spread everywhere a deadly contagion of typhus fever.   The famished survivors wandered through the villages devouring the most disgusting objects, and consuming even the corrupt bodies of animals.   The efforts of the Archbishop and his clergy were powerless to relieve the distress of the unfortunate, of whom nearly five hundred thousand died.   The government did not make known the scourge for fear of deterring new emigrants from locating in Algeria.   This silence was inhuman and culpable.

Archbishop Lavigerie, ignoring the political discretion of the Arabian Bureau and of the Administration, raised his voice in supplication to the charity of Europe.   He knew how to petition, for this was not his first attempt. He sent six priests throughout the whole world—to Europe, the United States, Canada—wherever he could

obtain alms. Although the Arabs were not of his faith, he was their father, and he felt obliged to alleviate their miseries. His eloquent and touching appeal found a response in every heart. To do good is not, however, sufficient, it must be done with intelligence and with a spirit of organization which multiplies the resources. He formed committees who sought out and relieved the most urgent cases, and who every day made an equal division of rations. Many families had entirely disappeared, others were abandoned without protection, and children wandered on the highways exposed to all the dangers which surround weakness, suffering, and inexperience.

One day in the month of November, 1867, a little child about ten years of age appeared at the door of the Archbishop. His intelligent but ghastly face wore a look of despair. "Where do you come from, my poor child?" asked the Archbishop. "From the mountains," replied the child, "far, far away." "And your parents" "My father," said he, "is dead, and my mother is in her gourbi (a cabin made of leaves)." "And why have you left her?" "We had no bread," he answered; "she told me to come to the Christian villages, and I have come. On the road, I lived on the grass and slept in the holes, so that the Arabs might not see me, because I was told that they kill children and eat them. The Arab priests set their dogs on me, and I do not wish to go to them again." "Ah, well," added the Archbishop, "come with me; you shall be one of my children, and you shall have my name." These children of the Archbishop were the pupils of the school of St. Eugene, to which the unfortunate little Arab was welcomed as a brother. A hundred

and twenty others applied for admission.   Childhood has
the power of exciting pity, but unfortunate childhood has
a particular claim on our compassion and love.   The Archbishop placed his trust in Providence, and interceded
everywhere for his orphans whom he could not turn into
the street.

During the famine he received almost two thousand
children, many of whom had been so sadly neglected,
that notwithstanding the care of the nurses five hundred
died.   After the famine some were restored to their
parents, whilst others were adopted by the Archbishop
and Catholic charity, and a permanent and regular tax
was levied for their maintenance.   The boys were placed
at Maison Carree under the direction of the Brothers, and
the girls at Kouba under the Sisters.   The alms received
from all parts of the world were set aside for the erection
of Arabian orphanages.   But the means of subsistence
could be obtained only by labor and the cultivation of the
soil, which has not only a lucrative but also a refining
effect.   The friends of the Archbishop argued that the
natural tendency of the Arabs to the nomadic life would
create difficulties and insurmountable obstacles, but he
was a man of action, and preferred to demonstrate by
experience rather than by arguments the merits of his
system.   The uncultivated lands were cleared and transformed into vineyards, cornfields and vegetable gardens.
The children roamed through the fields, and none ever
attempted to escape from the hospitable home which
sheltered them.   Some returned to their tribes, and
others remained of their free will to accustom themselves
to domestic life and labor.   In time the young men of

the orphanage intermarried with the girls at the Sisters, and thus was laid the foundation of Christian villages on the site of the ancient Roman colonies. The Archbishop, in his fatherly affection, distributed to each family a small house, a garden and some uncultivated land.

Such was the happy lot of the orphans, and such the origin of the villages of St. Cyprian and St. Monica. If a stranger were to inquire from an Arab the name of this village with its beautiful white houses and its cultivated gardens of vegetables and flowers, he would be told that this was 'the village of the Christian priest's sons;" and the Archbishop was indeed the father of the colony. So absolute was the confidence of his children in him that they received willingly from his hand their life companions. "Father," said a young man to him, "I wish to marry." "Well, my child," replied the Archbishop, "whom do you wish to marry?" "Oh, whomever you wish," said the young man. "But, my child," added the Archbishop, ".you should know"—he was not allowed to conclude the sentence. "You know very well," objected the young mam, "how to manage all that; I will be satisfied if you select the best girl for me." It is not necessary to add that the Archbishop never abused this confidence which was reposed in him, nor restrained by undue means the religious sentiments of the Arabian orphans. They were, however, instructed in the truths of Christianity, but no child was forced to accept the truth. Baptism was administered to children who were in danger of death, and this has ever been the custom of missioners in infidel countries. This system of education and of Christian assimilation bore, in time, abundant fruit.

The natural disposition of the Arabian children for adoration, prayer, and for whatever pertains to exterior worship disposed them towards Christian civilization. Archbishop Lavigerie has often recounted the consolations of his apostolate. "One day," he said, "an orphan about twelve years of age was sick at Ben-Aknoun. The Sisters placed him in the sick room, and when I called at the orphanage I stopped at his bed. He placed his hand on his breast and said to me: "I am all black inside." "Why, what do you mean, my child, I asked?" "My heart is black," he answered, "for I am not a child of God, and I want you to give me that water which makes the soul white before God and opens the gates of heaven." When he had been baptized, he asked for the "Bread of Life," and I readily consented to his pious request. At the sight of the Sacred Host that ghastly face lit up with the light of faith and love, a light which' seemed to transform his very features. He stretched his little emaciated hands towards the Sacred Host, and when he had received his first Holy Communion, he remained as in an ecstacy; his figure was truly transformed, and he became an apostle on his death-bed. "I am going to heaven to see Jesus," he said to me, and shortly afterwards he expired.

This success amongst the Arabs did not, however, modify the views of the government, which labored rather for Mahometan propagandism than for Christian proselytism. In consideration for the delicate consciences of the Arabs, the Administration ordered the Sisters to remove the Crucifix from the rooms of the hospitals, a command which they refused to obey. The French government supported

in Algeria many Mahometan schools and three Mahometan seminaries, which, according to an official report of
1864, numbered three thousand nine hundred students,
who were taught reading, writing, arithmetic, and the
Coran.   This self-styled tolerance converted the hatred of
the Arabians into scorn and contempt, for they enjoyed
the ridiculous conduct of a Catholic nation which annually
transported to Mecca hundreds of pilgrims who returned
from the holy city with an intense hatred for France and
for the name of Christian.   Sincere Mussulmans despised
these strangers who with their wavering convictions would
enter the mosque, as did General Desveux, and there
render public praise to Islam, and exhort the believers to
thank Providence for the innumerable benefits which
France had showered on them.

Marshal MacMahon had given Archbishop Lavigerie a
glimpse of the obstacles and difficulties of Algeria, but he
had not foreseen that from the Archbishop would come
the signal for warfare. The success of the Arabian orphanages had overthrown the argument of the government, for
the natives were susceptible to religion and to civilization.
The army was powerful, but the Catholic clergy with only
the force of persuasion wielded more power. The authorities began openly to oppose the Archbishop, who, they
said, took advantage of the miserable condition of the
Arabs by forcing them to accept either Baptism or death
by starvation.   This conduct was more culpable than the
dastardly act of the highwayman who forces the traveler
to yield up his purse.   The orphans who were imprisoned
by the Brothers and the Sisters would always keep alive
that distrust of the vanquished towards their conquerors.

Such absurd and calumnious reports reached the Governor-General, who was imbued with the prejudices of the Administration. He ordered the Archbishop to close the orphanages, and to return the children to their tribes.

A father does not, however, willingly allow his children to be carried off. The reply of the Archbishop to Marshal MacMahon was reproduced in the journals of the day. " It is said that I wish to force these poor Arabian children to sacrifice their religion for the mouthful of bread which Catholic charity has given them. No, Marshal ; this conduct would be unworthy of a bishop. I have never influenced the belief of the children whom I have relieved, nor have I baptized them except when they were in danger of death, and not even then without their consent if they had attained the use of reason. I shall always give them my paternal support, although they may decide in favor of the Mahommetan religion. I shall teach them, for I can teach only what I myself know, I shall teach them that it is better to provide by industry against the frowns of fortune than to drift slowly towards death while invoking destiny ; that it is better to rear a family than to live in the perpetual and shameful debauchery of divorce and polygamy; that it is better to love one another without distinction of race or creed than to kill '*the dogs of Christians;*' that France and her sovereigns are greater before God and man than the Turks and the Sultan. This is what I teach them, and who dares find fault with this method ? You know that I live in the most profound retirement and solitude, cut off from the world, and engaged only with my episcopal duties. If, then, the people of Algeria are drawn more closely towards me, it is because they consider my ideas and principles their only harbor of safety from the tempests which surround them."

" But I delay over details, whilst your letter has a higher import. It is the consequence of a false system. The Administration wishes to surround the natives of Algeria with barriers which, however, cannot impede the operation of the Church. This false system goes back even to the conquest. The first Archbishop of Algiers was abandoned by the Government and obliged to flee this land which he had watered with his tears and his blood, and had not the Prince, who to-day is the sovereign of France, generously aided him, he would have died in close confinement. Yes, it is well known that this noble apostle, who laid the foundation of many projects of religious hospitality, was persecuted by his rapacious creditors. And his successor, Archbishop Pavy, was not less unhappy. He was allowed no intercourse with the Arabians, and the venerable superior of his seminary was threatened with imprisonment and the galleys for having rescued two small Arabian children from the gutters of Algiers."

"And whilst the liberties of my venerable predecessors were thus curtailed, the government was erecting at much cost useless mosques, and by its protection of native schools was inciting religious fanaticism. What seems incredible, it authorized in the name of France, the study of the Coran, even amongst people who had never heard of it. Shall I multiply proofs? Notwithstanding the permission which was kindly given to me, I was not allowed to establish at my own expense, a house at Kabyle where the Sisters might distribute medicine and alms to the poor people. When the famine spread its ravages over Algeria,

I wished to assert my rights by throwing open my doors
to the native orphans.   I did so, and immediately words
of alarm rang through my ears, words which threatened
the future of my orphanages.   These words came true
when at the installation of the Brothers at Ben-Aknoun,
you publicly said that after the harvest you would send
back the orphans to their respective tribes, and close the
doors of the orphanages.   You imply, Marshal, that we
who have collected these forsaken fatherless children, and
who have placed them under the care of our religious
Brothers and Sisters, shall be obliged after some months
to set them at liberty, without protection, without defense,
a prey to the brutal passions of their co religionists.
Never! I would rather a thousand times their death!
You think this step necessary?   If you dare this deed, I
shall brand you before the world.   I would willingly
return these children to their parents and guardians, but
their parents and guardians are dead, and I am their
father and their protector.   They belong to me, for I
have preserved in them that life which animates them.
Force alone can snatch them from their asylum, and if
force be used I shall raise the indignation of all who have
in their hearts one spark of humanity or of Christianity."

"Two accusations are brought against me.   I have
raised too high the gloomy veil which concealed from the
eyes of France the evils of Algeria.   If this be a crime,
then I stand guilty.   I could not relieve the sufferings of
so many victims without an appeal to Christian charity.   I
am accused of exercising and of claiming a privilege
which comes to me from the Church and from truth—a
privilege conceded by civil law, and which henceforth will

be necessary for the safety of Algeria ; I mean the privilege of the Christian apostolate as I have defined it—the liberty which our priests require for the exercise of their zeal and charity among the Arabians. If this be a fault, I am guilty ; and now I increase my guilt by demanding for my priests the right of performing their duty in an infidel country where only dangers and perils await them. I know by this demand that I wish to overthrow the present system of the Arabian Bureau, by removing the barriers which separate us from the natives. But whither has this system of the Arabian Bureau conducted us ?"

" I recognize the noble valor of the army in the plains, the valleys, and the mountains; our soldiers have covered themselves with immortal glory. I speak not of the army nor of the military authorities, but of that system by which the Administration regulates our intercourse with the Arabians. *Politically*, we have as many enemies as at the time of the conquest. You yourself told me that you opposed the spread of Christianity for fear of exciting the fanaticism of the Arabs, for in case of a war with Europe you could not count on the fidelity of twenty natives. *Economically*, the Arabian tribes have been for five months the prey to a famine from which they will not recover for several years. *Morally*, the Arabians have imbibed our vices, but not our good qualities, and they have become absolutely rebellious to all progress. And this is the result of a sway of thirty-eight years under Catholic France! It is time then to discard that system which has been condemned by God and by man. And if momentary inconveniences arise from this effort, what are inconveniences and sacrifices in comparison with the present failure? Algeria does not rest upon the solid foundation of Christian civilization."

The Archbishop was not satisfied with this indignant protest to the Governor-General. He hastened to plead before Napoleon III a cause which was so vital to the interests of France. "The Algerian government," he said, "endeavors to conceal and to misrepresent the miseries of the Arabians. These miseries and the incredible indifference of the Arabs towards the government have forced upon all enlightened inhabitants of the colonies the conviction that the only means of safety lies in a rapid and a complete assimulation of the Arabians with the Christians. Sire, the time has arrived for the development of that moral and religious training. Allow us then to exert at least the influence of our charity and zeal."

This appeal touched the Emperor, who felt that although the Archbishop was rather positive in his opinions, he was an exemplary bishop, a true patriot, and a zealous advocate of the truth. He resolved to compromise matters by offering him a prominent diocese in France as a recompense for his noble exertions in Algeria; but he knew not his man, for Archbishop Lavigerie was never attracted by the glitter of personal ambition. "Sire," he replied, "I am thankful for your kind proposal; but were I to accept, it would be to my own and to the Church's dishonor." His firmness and his disinterestedness were victorious, for the Emperor gave him full permision to continue his work of love amongst the orphans. Marshal MacMahon was replaced by Admiral De Gueydon, who embraced the views of Archbishop Lavigerie, and ably seconded him in his apostolate amongst the Arabians.

CHAPTER IX.

THE WHITE FATHERS OF ALGIERS—THE WHITE SIS-
TERS—THE VATICAN COUNCIL—THE WAR—
THE FRENCH DEPUTIES.

By a royal grant absolute freedom was given to the Archbishop in the management of his works, and he now entered into a project for the present and the future protection of his orphans. The foreign congregations which were engaged in his diocese could assure him only temporary assistance, whilst the colonial clergy had made no advance in their relations with the Arabians. He resolved to organize a distinct congregation, whose mission would be the evangelization of the natives. The saintly Father Gerard, of the congregation of the Lazarists, and superior of the seminary of Kouba, was instrumental in effecting this object, and he lived to see the complete assimilation of the natives and the clergy. The charity of his holy founder, St. Vincent de Paul, was revived in him, and he labored to infuse into his students a zeal and love for souls. One day in the year 1868 he presented to the Archbishop three youths. "Your Grace," he said, "here are three youths who wish to devote themselves to the African Apostolate With God's grace this will be the beginning of the work." The many occupations of the Archbishop prevented him from undertaking their formation in the religious life, but Divine Providence came to his aid.

Two French priests, R. P. Vincent and M. Gillet, the
Director of the Seminary of Nantes, applied for adoption.
The Archbishop saw the necessity of placing the students
in an apartment distinct from the large seminary, and a
religious and a secular priest had come to his assistance.
A religious of the Company of Jesus undertook the direction of the novitiate.   The question of location and of
money was of no consequence.   A house was procured
on the heights of El-Biarr, as the permanent abode of the
five members, but the community increased so rapidly
that the Archbishop was forced to seek a more commo-
dious building.   St. Eugene, the former residence of the
French Consul, had been transformed by Archbishop
Pavy into a preparatory seminary, or rather into a mixed
school in which youths not destined for the eclesiastical
state were also educated.   The large buildings of the
seminary at Kouba sheltered also the students of St.
Eugene, and this latter establishment became an apostolic
school in which were installed the students for the African
missions.

By an ingenious stroke of policy, the Archbishop
decided that the missioners to the Arabians should wear
the same costume as their future neophytes ; and naturally they were designated by their white habit as the
White Fathers.   The novitiate was soon filled by
numerous recruits from France, Belgium and Holland,
who had hastened to this field of labor in the hope of
finding amongst the fanatical Mussulmans and the poor
negro slaves an outlet for their zeal.   The Archbishop
resolved to transfer the novitiate of the White Fathers
to the Maison-Carree, where a large tract of land had

been cleared and cultivated by the orphans. In 1873, the Provincial Council of Algiers, by a special decree, which received the approbation of the Holy See, publicly encouraged and sanctioned the new congregation. Six years after the institution of the congregation, the founder convoked a general chapter for the election of the first superior. The White Fathers wished to confer this honor on the Archbishop, but he absolutely declined. He saw the inconveniences of such a mode of government, for a member of the secular clergy could not usefully govern a congregation of religious. Father Dugerry, a nephew of the heroic pastor of the Madeline who was assassinated during the Commune, was chosen superior, a· position which he repeatedly held, until his humble supplications and his bodily infirmities induced the Fathers to look elsewhere for a superior. The White Fathers are at present exempt from the jurisdiction of the ordinary, and are subject to the Apostolic Delegate for the mission of the Sahara and the Soudan.

Christian charity had invented no means of reaching the Arabian women, for Arabian etiquette forbade men to enter the harem. A congregation of religious women devoted to works of charity amongst these poor female slaves was the next thought of the Archbishop, and the difficulty of such an undertaking only stimulated his zeal. He placed the postulants for this work under the direction of the Sisters of St. Charles, and the Sisters of the Assumption, who had recently emigrated from France. After a religious training of ten years, the·novices were formed into an independent congregation ; and the White Sisters completed and perfected the labors of the White

Fathers. Their duties were clearly defined. They would instruct the infidel women in the first principles of the Christian religion, open boarding schools for the natives and for the Christian children, conduct the hospitals and the orphanages and labor for the education and the protection of the poor Arabians.

We may easily imagine the feelings which this evangelical charity excited in the hearts of the Arabian people. In the East, woman is despised ; she is condemned to the most arduous labor; she becomes the slave and servant of man, a beast of burden, a creature of an inferior class who has no claim to his esteem nor his kindness, much less to his affection. The exertions of the humble religious won the admiration and the love of these unfortunate women, who considered them supernatural beings sent from heaven. The Archbishop frequently repeated the remark of an old Mussulman to one of the Sisters of Charity : "Sister," he said, "when you and the other religious descended from heaven, were you clothed as you are now ?" The poor Arabians considered nothing impossible to these noble women who had abandoned everything for God and the service of the unfortunate. One day three White Sisters went to a village in which there was much sickness. The inhabitants were urgent in their demands, but the cries and the importunities of one woman attracted the Sisters. "Come with me, come with me !" she supplicated. "I will go," replied the Sister, "when I attend to these sick." "No ! come immediately," cried the mother, "you must cure my son." "What is wrong with him ?" asked the Sister. "He is dead," sobbed the mother. Poor pagan woman. She thought that even death should recoil before the skill and the devotion of the Catholic religious.

In the midst of these new labors, the voice of the Pope resounded over the world calling the Bishops to the Vatican Council. Archbishop Lavigerie set out for Rome, but a sad scene there awaited him, for his friend, Archbishop Maret, of Lepano, the former Dean of the Sarbonne, opposed the Papal Infallibility, and the two suffragans, Bishop Callop, of Oran, and Bishop Las Casas, of Constantine, pronounced against the seasonableness of the definition ; but he himself held aloof from every faction. It pained him to hold convictions contrary to the opinion and the sentiments of his former dean, but friendship could not warp his judgment nor his convictions. The Cardinal Secretary of State, to whom Pius IX one day remarked, "And the Archbishop of Algiers, how does he act ? " could happily reply, " Like an angel, Most Holy Father." The Pope had not an opportunity of congratulating him on his attitude, for two days after the dogmatic definition, a new sensation fell like a thunder clap on the civilized world ; two great powers, Prussia and France, had rushed to arms, and war was declared. This event dispersed the Council, for all the bishops hastened back to their dioceses.

The announcement of the disaster of his country found a sad echo in the heart of the Archbishop, but he did not succumb to fruitless lamentation. With his practical turn of mind and his knowledge of the needs of the situation he desired to remedy the terrible evils of war. He endeavored to retrieve the miseries of his puor compatriots, the inhabitants of Alsace and Lorraine, those children of his first apostolate, many of whom he had

held in his arms.   He offered them the hospitality of that
Algerian soil, which he so dearly cherished, and whose
resources he well knew.   He appealed to them, he urged
them, he detailed with a paternal solicitude the advantages
of emigration from the devastations which the annexation
of 1870 had caused.   He lauded the charms of the country,
and the salubrious climate, which surpassed even that of
Alsace.   He begged the poor farmers to water with the
sweat of their brow the fertile fields of "African France."
He entered into details.   "Come," he said to them, "the
State will sell to you at a moderate price thousands of
acres of land, the payment of which will not be required
until you are in comfortable circumstances.   I, who have
been your bishop, tell you this, and it would be a crime to
deceive you.   I do not know one laborious and sober
family, for these requisites are absolutely necessary, which
would not shortly be well repaid."   He then reassured
them of the religious advantages of Algeria.   "Come,
the Sisters who instruct the children, and care for the poor
and the sick, are almost all from Lorraine and Alsace.
There are about five hundred Sisters of Christian Doctrine
from Nancy and Provence.   You will have these friends
to bid you welcome to Algeria.   Come, and you will learn
to love, as they do, this land on which God has showered
his gifts."

During the entire war he donated to the Republic part
of his salary for the purchase of arms, and he said to his
diocesans: "You will pardon your bishop, if he now
curtails the exterior marks of his dignity, and if he thus
gives you the example in this sad trial of his country."
He offered the bells of his cathedral and of the other

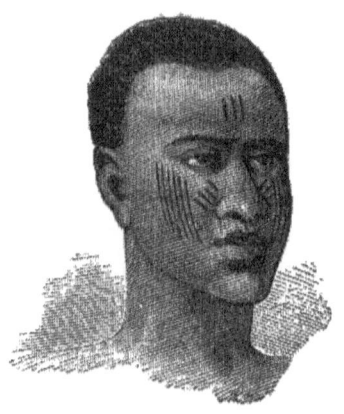

TYPES FOUND ON THE UPPER NIGER.

churches for the construction of cannons for France; and in the many insurrections which arose in Algiers, he encouraged the clergy to manifest openly their patriotism. He, himself, assisted at the solemn obsequies of the parish priest of Palestra, who had been killed whilst defending his parishoners; and he showed special marks of attention to Father Gillard, who had been wounded by the bursting of a shell at Sedan. He went to meet him on his return, and forthwith appointed him Vicar General of the diocese.

The devil constantly finds men prepared to work out his designs by opposing the advance of Christianity; and the Administration was the ready instrument in the hands of the author of evil. The co-operation of Admiral De Gueydon gave a respite from the persecution of the Arabian Bureau, but this respite was of short duration. The Admiral was replaced by General Chanzy, a brave and loyal soldier, who from the first was the object of calumny. The acknowledgment is shameful, but conceal-ment would be cowardice; it was France that conspired against its own interests in Algeria, and religious hatred shortly raised its hideous head. Since the conquest, religious ceremonies had been performed publicly, and the procession of the Blessed Sacrament on the Feast of Corpus Christi was attended with extraordinary solemnity. The civil and the military authorities assisted. Benediction was given at the public departments, and even those governors who, as Marshal Randon, belonged to the reformed religion, were present with their staff; it was a noble manifestation of the national worship of France. In 1872, an edict emanating from the municipal council of Algiers suppressed the processions, against which tyrannical measure the Archbishop vigorously protested. He summoned all the pastors with their parishoners, schools and societies, to take part in a public procession around the Church of "Our Lady of Africa." The land which bordered on this pious sanctuary was the property of the church, and hence no one could prevent a ceremony which was interdicted on the streets of the metropolis. This energetic resistance enraged the Sectarians and forced them to a new resource.

Although the Catholic works of Africa were under the management of the Archbishop of Algiers, the advance of religion was greatly facilitated by a governmental subsidy of twenty thousand dollars which was appropriated annually for Algeria. This money, which contributed not a little towards that love and esteem of the Arabians for the name of France, was utilized for the orphans, the seminaries, and the various works of charity. A journalist by the name of Warnier, who had at first admired the Archbishop and encouraged his undertakings, blinded by his political success, abjured the past, and made an open attack against the actions of the Prelate. According to the habitual tactics of those who dare not state facts nor cite witnesses who may belie their words, Warnier announced to France that Archbishop Dupech had in confidence condemned the conduct of the Archbishop of Algiers. Moreover, the Arabian Bureau had accused him of exerting that influence which he had gained over the Arabians, not for the profit of France, but for his own profit. Soon he would be the great elector of Algeria, with the sum of twenty thousand dollars at his disposal, to utilize to the detriment of the public good. This subsidy should, by all means, be withheld. Thus the plot was laid.

The surprise and indignation of the Archbishop at the language of the writer found vent in a reply. The attack had been public, the reply should be public. He dispatched to all the deputies a letter in which he alluded to the approval lately given to his works by this journalist, and he concluded with these words: "When renegades attack our work, it is well to inform Çatholic France that the future of Algeria belongs neither to the Arabians nor to the Mussulmans." That year the credit was continued, but the bitter hatred was not disarmed, and the following year the government withheld the subsidy. The grants which had been made to the clergy and to the seminaries were discussed in open council, and to the scandal of all true Christian and patriotic men, they also were reduced to a nominal sum.

Universal suffrage is a beautiful thing, but that modern liberty which is so rooted in our customs and manners often gives rise to adverse criticism. The Chamber of Deputies during one year encroaches upon every religious, political, scientific and administrative question. This supposes in each member certain qualities which belong equally to the elector, for it is he who selects the representative of the majority. In a word, universal suffrage implies universal knowledge and savors much of optimism. Catholic electors should act conscientiously. They should be guided by an inflexible attachment to principle, and not by personal sympathy, in their selection of deputies who perhaps are honest in public life, but who have neither the education nor the capability of deciding affairs of grave importance. These deputies too often cast their votes without considering the gravity of their act, or the disastrous consequences. In 1876, the French Chamber of Deputies, without mature reflection, suppressed fifty thousand dollars of the two hundred thousand which had been appropriated for the advance of religion in Algeria. The general council of Algiers readily imitated the example of the French Deputies, and they suppressed the grants which had been accorded to religious works. The French Catholics advocated this measure, whilst the Mussulmans, followers of Mahomet, through their admiration for Archbishop Lavigerie, unanimously voted for the continuence of the appropriation. This withdrawal did not dampen the ardor of the Archbishop, for he resolved to evangelize not only Algeria, but the entire African Continent.

CHAPTER X.

THE FIRST EXPLORERS, LIVINGSTONE, STANLEY AND PAUL DE BRAZZA—THE EVANGELIZATION OF AFRICA IN THE NINETEENTH CENTURY.

In a cotton factory at Blantyre, Scotland, at the beginning of this century, was a young boy who read with avidity whatever books his poor earnings could supply. He spent his evenings in deep study and composition, and finally he passed from the cotton factory to the medical college of Glasgow. This prodigious student, who by his natural energy and perseverance became a learned man, was David Livingstone, the great explorer of Africa.

He was not a Catholic, but his tender and compassionate
heart was fired with the ardent and the generous zeal of a
Catholic missioner. His researches in the field of history
aroused his interest in the poor Africans who were plunged
into the depths of paganism and barbarity, and he resolved
to win them to civilization and to the truths of the Gospel.

In 1840, the London Missionary Society furnished him
with the necessary means, and after a voyage of three
months he landed at Cape Town. He took up his residence four hundred miles inland amongst the Bakwain
tribe, whose king, Sechele, embraced Christianity, with
all his tribe. Encouraged by this success, he started with
his wife and children, in 1849, for the Kalahara desert, but
the African fevers, the absence of water, and the decep-
tive mirage of Lake Ngama, forced him to return and
seek some months rest with the Bakwains. In 1851, he
departed for the country of the Makololos. Sebituane,
the king of the country, joyfully welcomed the Christian
religion, and in his last moments he was consoled by the
pious exhortations of Livingstone, who taught him the
value of the soul, and the happiness of the life beyond the
grave. The explorer, however, expressed a melancholy
regret that he could not give to the chief the solace of the
Catholic religion. "I never before felt so grieved," he
writes in his journal, "by the loss of a black man, and it
was impossible not to follow him in thought into the
world of which he had just heard before he was called
away, and to realize somewhat of the feeling of *those who
pray for the dead.*"

In 1852, he undertook his third voyage, which established his reputation throughout the civilized world. After

a difficult journey towards the north through a gigantic
and unknown forest, he arrived by this new route in the
country of the Makololos, who willingly seconded him in
his expedition, and furnished him with an escort as far as
Saint Paul de Loanda.   This trying voyage completely
exhausted his strength. " Never shall I forget," he writes,
" the luxurious pleasure which I enjoyed on feeling
myself again in a good English couch, after having slept
on the ground for six months."   He accomplished a great
work by this expedition, for he established the possibility
of intercourse between the nations of the East and the
interior of Africa.   He departed for England in the company of Sekwehe, his faithful Makololo guide.   " What
a strange country this is," said the guide at the sight of
the ocean, " all water, water everywhere ! "   But this
sight of an immense expanse of water confused the mind
of the poor African, and in a fit of frenzy he cast himself
overboard.

In 1859, Livingstone began his exploration of the
mouths and the tributaries of the great cataracts of the
Zambesi river, with a view of utilizing them for the spread
of commerce and of religion.   It was in the neighborhood of Lake Nyassa that he first witnessed the horrors
of the Negro slave trade, in which many Portuguese
traders were engaged.   On his return to London in 1864,
one of the Queen's counsellors asked him what recompense he wished for his valuable service.   This generous
and disinterested hero replied : " For myself I wish nothing, but you will reward me beyond measure if you check
that disgraceful traffic by which the Portuguese carry the
Negroes of Africa into slavery."

The following year the London Geographical Society sent him in search of the sources of the river Nile, and on this voyage he saw the Arabian Mussulmans vieing with the Portuguese of Zambesi in their ferocious pursuit of the slave trade. He continued the exploration of Lake Nyassa, and discovered Lake Moero and Lake Bangweolo, but he arrived at Ujiji, on the shores of Lake Tanganyika, in a state of complete exhaustion, and although he was suffering from severe pains of the lungs, he discovered, May 31, 1871, not the sources of the Nile, but of the Loualaba, that is the Congo, one of the most important rivers of the African Continent.

Whilst he was pursuing this prodigious voyage, the report of his death flashed through the continent. It had been announced to the Consul at Zanzibar that most of his servants had deserted him, and that he had been killed by a savage tribe. The Geographical Society, which had not heard from him for two years, immediately organized an expedition ; but Henry M. Stanley, a correspondent for the "New York Herald," had anticipated this action of the Society. On November 16, 1871, he was sent by James Gordan Bennett, Jr., at an expense of twenty-five thousand dollars, to obtain accurate information about Livingstone if living, and if dead, to bring home his remains. He joined the explorer at Ujiji, and after three months he returned laden with precise geographical directions concerning the course of the streams of the African mountains. Livingstone bravely continued his explorations, and in January, 1873, he arrived on the western shore of Lake Tanganyika, but in so exhausted a condition that he was borne on a litter to the village of Chitambo, where he calmly and peacefully expired. His heart was buried in the village, and his body was embalmed and carried to Zanzibar, then across the ocean to the shores of his native land, and amid tokens of mourning and admiration such as England accords only to her greatest sons, it was interred in Westminster Abbey.

The impartial historian entwines with the names of Livingstone and Stanley, the name of Paul de Brazza Savorgnan, to whom France owes an immense debt of gratitude. He was born in Rome, in 1852, and received his education in Paris. After having passed a brilliant examination in which he displayed superior intelligence, great energy and an ardent imagination, he was admitted into the French navy. He served in Africa on the Gaboon station, and under the command of Admiral de Quillio, he made a voyage on the western part of Africa. He had often heard the French merchants complain of that excessive competition which each day depreciated the commercial market, and he resolved to penetrate the interior of Africa, that he might discover a new channel for the increase of French industry. In 1878, he became an ensign on board the vessel *Venus*, which coasted along the Gaboon region. He obtained the permission of his superior to land with some sailors, and after a short march to the north of the Congo river, he arrived in the kingdom of a powerful savage tribe. The king, Makoko, was so influenced by the force of Brazza's persuasion that he made a solemn treaty, October 3, 1880, in which he placed his states under the protection of France, and a railway which was constructed between Brazzaville and the coast, opened immense territories for the commercial interests of France.

These details on the first explorers of Africa are not a digression, for they enable us to appreciate the eminently religious and patriotic work of the Archbishop of Algiers. He had long foreseen that Europe would advance slowly and surely to the subjugation of these rich and extensive countries, and that heresy would strive for the conversion of the natives. During his entire life his one ambition was the propagation of the true faith and the patriotic development of his country's interests. The religious civilization of the devout and zealous protestant, Livingstone, had not gained a secure foothold in Africa, but noble Catholic missioners had implanted the Cross of Christ at different points of the African coast, and many of them had suffered death for their faith.

The frivolous and egotistic world which believes neither in sacrifice nor in self-oblation should know the names of some of those obscure heroes who so generously gave their lives for the spread of the Gospel. Before 1864, Christianity in Africa was limited in the east to the Vicariate of Egypt and the Prefecture of Abyssinia; in the west, to the two Guineas; and in the interior, to the Mountains of the Moon, a Christian station at Cape Horn and Madagascar, to which island St. Vincent de Paul, at the request of Louis the XIV, had sent missioners. The Roman provinces of Egypt and Abyssinia had been evangelized in the fourth century by St. Frumentius, and the church which was founded by him preserved for five centuries the sacred deposit of faith. Amid the devastations which swept like a destructive tempest over Alexandria, that church stood as a monument to the young Abyssinian prince who had supplicated the King of Portugal for a

colony of Catholic missioners.   However, the fickle character of the Abyssinians and the fanaticism of heretical
monks prevented the lasting establishment of Catholicity
in that country.   The Jesuits and the Franciscans were in
turn protected or persecuted in proportion as a wise king
or a tyrant sat on the throne.

A learned Frenchman, Antonin d'Abaddie, who in 1843
had made an expedition through Abyssinia, wrote to his
friend, Charles de Montalembert, that "the Christian traditions which were there preserved rendered the task of
the missioner relatively easy."   The natives were so
desirous for priests that they seized a French traveler, who
they thought belonged to the ministry.   Their reason is
an evidence of ignorance and of good faith.   "This
stranger," said they, "is not a woman, hence he is holy ;
he knows how to read, hence he is a priest ; he is white,
hence he is a bishop, and he will consecrate the priests
that we desire."   Father Leon des Avanchens, who was
sent to Abyssinia in 1851, says that he met many native
Mussulmans who observed as a sacred inheritance from
their fathers the feasts of Easter, Pentecost, the Ascension
and the Assumption ; but these remnants of Christianity
were mingled with many pagan practices.   The importance
of the Abyssinian mission does not consist in the number
of its neophytes, but in the necessity of controlling for
Catholicity a means of communication with Central Africa.
The Mussulmans, who carefully guard the coast of Africa,
have informed the inhabitants of the interior that the
religion of Mahomet is the true and the only religion, and
they know that Catholicism has serious motives in holding
this key to the unexplored regions.

The first missioners of Madagascar were sent at the suggestion of Louis XIV, who contemplated the subjugation of that island. The inhabitants welcomed the truths of Christianity, and soon the labors of the mission were so arduous and the neophytes so numerous that these apostles were obliged to beg the assistance of additional missioners. To-day this flourishing mission is under the spiritual direction of the Jesuit Fathers.

The idea of evangelizing Central Africa originated with a Polish Jesuit, Father Maximillian Ryllo. Whilst in Syria he had formed the acquaintance of a merchant who had traveled in the region of the Soudan, and he concluded that a country which could be penetrated for the interests of gain or of commerce, was open also to the saving truths of the Catholic Church. In 1846, whilst Rector of the Propaganda, he obtained from Gregory XVI a brief creating him Vicar Apostolic over the new mission of Central Africa. In 1848 he departed for Khartum with four Italian missioners, but he died shortly afterwards, leaving his charge to Mgr. Knoblecher, of the diocese of Laybach. The new Vicar Apostolic interested Francis II, the Emperor of Austria, in the undertaking, and owing to the reinforcement of some Italian Jesuits and pecuniary assistance from Germany, he was enabled to penetrate the country. But the poor missioners succumbed to the rigors of the climate, and in 1871 the stations of Khartum, Kondoraka, Sante-Crux and Sculla had cost the lives of forty priests. One of the survivors, Daniel Comboni, bravely pursued his labors, with the aid of the religious of the Order of Saint Camillus de Lellis, who penetrated the northern part of Central Africa. Mgr. Barrou, the Vicar

Apostolic of the two Guineas, obtained from the founder
of the Holy Ghost Order seven priests and three brothers,
who sailed from France in 1843; but with the exception
of Father Bessieux and a brother, they were all overcome
by fever and died.   Two years later, Father Bessieux was
appointed Bishop of Galliopolis, with Bishop Kobet as his
coadjutor.   From this period the Holy Ghost Fathers
evangelized the coast of Guinea, but were unable to penetrate the interior, which was carefully guarded by the
Mahometan slave-dealers.

In opposition to every human and divine law, many
half-breeds were engaged in the repulsive traffic of Negro
slavery, and they opposed whatever might destroy this
lucrative commerce, especially an invasion of the Europeans.
In 1871, Father Comboni sent the following information
to the Central Council for the Propagation of the Faith :
" In Egypt, every family that is not too poor owns a Negro
or a Negress.   Many families have two slaves, and the
rich in proportion to their wealth.   Europeans are of the
opinion that Negro slavery is a crime of the past, but I
can affirm that this ignoble traffic exists in all Egypt.   Of
late years the public markets are closed, but the Negroes
are driven like a herd of animals into the smaller locali-
ties.   I myself have been asked to buy Negro slaves, and
I can point out the city of Bulhar in which every fifteen
days Negroes are publicly sold.   These unhappy creatures
are brought from the centre of Africa, where the inhuman
cupidity of the cruel speculator has led him to penetrate.
Children are stolen from the fields and from the banks of
the rivers, and are separated forever from their homes.
After the perils of a long voyage through the treacherous

desert of Korasko, they are thrown into a large vessel laden with gum and elephants' tusks. There they are crowded, without distinction of sex, without regard for disease, with a nourishment more to the taste of animals than to human beings. They are secretly landed at Bulhar, where they are surrounded by purchasers, who carefully examine their qualities. If they are strong and healthy, they are sold for a hundred to a hundred and twenty-five dollars."

It remained for a great Frenchman, the Primate of Africa and Archbishop of Algiers, to raise the cry of alarm and to denounce to the civilized world this curse of Africa. Hitherto the attempts to penetrate the interior of Africa had only been private—each nation or each learned society had followed its own views. But, in 1876, in consequence of the publication of the travels of Livingstone and Stanley, the king of Belgium matured the idea of an international association for the purpose of opening to civilization the undiscovered parts of Africa. The Congress of Brussels made a great display, and this crusade against barbarity attracted many an ambitious youth. They proposed to establish at the most important points of the country centres of exploration and of scientific research, and the Belgium explorers wished to erect a line of communication between Zanzibar and Lake Tanganyika. This idea was great and noble, but whilst the traveler, the scholar, and the merchant would profit by the route to Equitorial Africa, the interests of religion were ignored. Although the members of the international association, who were for the most part Protestant, did not directly oppose the spread of the Gospel, they announced in their program that their efforts would tend principally to the advancement of science, commerce and industry.

This was the aspect which, in 1877, the question of
Equitorial Africa assumed before the Christian world and
before the Holy See. Cardinal Franchi, the Prefect of the
Propaganda, called the attention of the Holy Father to the
result of the conference of Brussels. The interior of Africa
had been pictured as a vast desert, so sterile that habita-
tion was impossible, but the reports of the courageous dis-
coverers and of the missioners had dispelled these false
historical and geographical ideas. That desert land—as
extensive in territory as Europe—was inhabited by a hundred million Negroes; those sterile deserts and barren
hills were fertile and productive lands and studded with
beautiful lakes; those inaccessible and lofty mountains
were covered with perpetual snows. The Protestant societies of London and of New York, electrified by the
accounts of Livingstone and Stanley, were planning con-
quests in this extensive and wealthy country, and the Conference of Brussels had added a new aspect to the crusade.
Should the Holy See remain inactive and allow the guardians of error to excel the apostles of truth and of civilization? Yet this vast and perilous mission presented a
practical difficulty. The religious societies of that apostolate were in need of missioners, for the treacherous climate
and fevers, and the burning heat of Abyssinia and Dahomey had every year destroyed a large number. Where,
then, were the laborers and the necessary resources for
the evangilization of those vast regions? Fortunately, a
remedy was at hand.

In 1876, Archbishop Lavigerie brought to Rome two
White Fathers of Algiers, the first fruits of his foundation.
The thought of the evangelization of Africa from the

North—that is, from Algeria, Tunis, and Tripoli—had long pre-occupied his mind, but he was a man who slowly matured his vast projects. The gate of Central Africa was Abyssinia, and he proposed to pass around this guarded entrance and to penetrate Central Africa from the South. In the supposition that communication could be established with the capital of the Soudan and the Niger river, why could he not ascend to the region of the lakes, to the source of the Nile and of the Congo, and even to Lake Tchad, in the heart of the Soudan? He was actuated mainly by a desire for spiritual conquest, but in the division of Africa amongst the European powers and in the development of the international congress, he wished France also to play her part. Pius IX. had only a vague and imperfect knowledge of the White Fathers whom Archbishop Lavigerie presented to him. "Ah," he said, "they are, then, Arabian priests?" "Not by birth," replied the Archbishop, "but by charity." "Are you disposed," added the Pope to them, "to become good missioners?" "Most Holy Father," they answered, "with God's grace, we will do what you wish." "They are prepared," said the Archbishop, "even for martyrdom, if God so wills. They are the first fruit of the African mission, and they desire to penetrate the interior. Send them on their journey, Most Holy Father, with your blessing, that they may have the strength to suffer, and, if necessary, to die for their faith." The Pope thoroughly appreciated the seasonable and generous offer of the White Fathers.

The mission cf Central Africa was ripe for the harvest, and in 1877, Pius IX asked the advice of the superiors of the principal missions on the advisability of founding new stations in the districts in which the African International Society was located. The prelates unanimously gave their approval to this step, and the Pope officially entrusted the task to the White Fathers. They responded with enthusiasm. All religious societies have their epochs of heroism; and this was the hour for the White Fathers. They dispatched two members to Rome to express their gratitude, and to place at the disposal of the Holy See their wills, their sufferings, and even their lives for the salvation of Equitorial Africa. The bearers of such beautiful sentiments arrived in Rome in 1878, but God had called the great and holy Pontiff to Himself. His successor, Leo XIII, obtained from the Propaganda the necessary expenses for the return of the missioners, and he assigned to the White Fathers four centres in which the conference of Brussels had proposed to establlsh stations: Lake Nyanza, Lake Tanganyika, the capital of Muata Yanva's kingdom, and the northern extremity of the Congo river. The Pontiff grasped the idea of Archbishop Lavigerie, and in order to forestall the advance of heresy, he ordered* the immediate departure of the missioners for the field of action.

CHAPTER XI.

THE WORK OF ARCHBISHOP LAVIGERIE IN EQUATORIAL AFRICA AND AT LAKE TANGANYIKA.

The Society of the White Fathers of "Our Lady of Africa" had been strengthened by the baptism of blood. Algerian missioners had been located at stations bordering

on the Sahara, at Biskra, Gerriville, Laghonat and
Metlili, and Fathers Paulmier, Menoret and Bouchand
had ventured into the Sahara with the expectation of
reaching the Soudan from the south, but they were
massacred by a band of fanatical Mussulmans. Fathers
Richards, Morat and Pouplard, unable to reach Timbuctoo by this perilous route, attempted to pass through
Tripoli, but they were attacked at Rhat and fell victims of
their zeal.

The Archbishop mourned the loss of his first sons, but
his practical mind profited by this sad occurrence to impress on his missioners the necessity of moderating their
zeal with Christian prudence. "My dear Sons," he said
to them, "let the exercise of your zeal be seasoned by
the virtues of prudence, patience and charity. Prudence,
for if you desire to hasten affairs, you will often endanger
yourselves without effecting any good. One imprudent
act may retard for a long time the conversion of many
people. Never lose sight of your sacred character nor
the spirit of your order which has a special end in view,
the absence of which would destroy its utility. You
must gain the attention of the natives by your language,
dress, mode of eating; in a word, by your conformity to
their customs. Other congregations may adopt different
methods, but you must faithfully cultivate the portion
which the Father of the family has entrusted to you."

He introduced into the constitution of the society precise instructions which gave strength to his general
remarks. "Never," he stated, "under any circumstances,
shall less than three priests be on a mission. The most
advantageous and urgent offers shall not make an excep-

tion to this rule, which is essential to the existence of the society." This measure provided for the spiritual and for the temporal welfare of the congregation, so that no member would be alone in a pagan country during life nor at the hour of death.

The Archbishop was prepared to make any sacrifice of money, for unless he wished to expose a missioner to certain death, he must equip him with an extensive outfit. The European traveler, who can quickly pass by railway from one end of the country to the other, cannot realize the hardship of a journey into Equatorial Africa. The best roads are only winding paths through thick undergrowth, frequented more by wild beasts than by man, and where two men cannot walk abreast. Then the baggage is not less complicated. Have you ever reflected on the inconveniences of travel in a country which has no currency? The traveler must carry the indispensable articles of life, or more cumbersome articles with which to procure them. How easily the price of sustenance in Europe may be placed in a small pocketbook? Only the missioner lost in the immense African forests can appreciate and mournfully meditate on the advantages of currency. There is everywhere a system of buying and of selling, but to buy with money is a necessity to which every one is resigned. In Africa there is no money, and its substitute is most cumbersome—cloth, glassware, brassware, knives, axes, mirrors; all these are less easily carried than a few bank notes. And it is not without effort that each man carries on his back at least seventy pounds of wares, and instead of a satchel and an umbrella, large packs of tents, hammocks and cooking utensils. And what security has he in his journey? Africa is overrun with hyenas, serpents, jackals, lions and other wild beasts, without mentioning the cannibals who, as in Dahomey, believe that they appease the gods by human sacrifices. This is neither exaggeration nor pessimism ; the letters of every missioner are a proof of its realty.

An instance is found in a letter of Father Baur, the Vica-Prefect Apostolic of Zanzibar, who traveled in the interior. "The white skins of the Europeans," he writes, "attracted the attention of the Wadoes, who had never seen a foreign caravan, and their reflections were not reassuring to the poor travelers.." "Look," said one of them, smacking his lips, "I think that fellow would be good to eat." "I would not like him,' replied another, he must be an Arabian ; but that large one who looks like a giraffe, he ought to be excellent." M. Durand wrote in his journal the following conversation between himself and one of the neophytes who one day appeared much dejected. "You seem sad, my friend," said the good priest, "tell me what is wrong." "Yes, I am sad," replied the savage, "I am very sad, for I did not have a good breakfast." "What did you eat ?" asked the priest, in a soothing tone. "Nothing, Father," he answered, "only two ears of a man, and how could I live on that ?" And it was to people of this class that Pope Leo XIII and Archbishop Lavigerie had sent the White Fathers.

On the 25th of March, 1878, five Fathers departed for Lake Tanganyika and five for Lake Nyanza. They were received at Zanzibar by the Holy Ghost Fathers, and there they prepared their caravan for Tabora. The kindness of Father Horer, the superior of the order, deeply

touched Father Livinhac, who wrote thus to Archbishop
Lavigerie : "Father Horer received us as a father receives
his children.   He is truly an apostolic man, and his confreres are all good and kind.   They requested us to par-
take of their hospitality during our visit."   Father Pascal,
the superior of the mission of Tanganyika contracted a
fever and died before he reached the end of his perilous
journey.   He spoke of his illness with the joyfulness of
a saint.   " I have been visited by our dear sister, the
fever," he writes from Kondora, "everybody has patiently
to bear his trials and sufferings.   But what a great consolation to suffer for the Good Master, and for those whom
he has redeemed by His precious blood!"   He was,
indeed, ripe for heaven.

His companions arrived at Tanganyika after a journey
of ten months, and the other missioners reached Nyanza,
one year, ten months and twenty-nine days after their
departure from Algiers.   The sting of a poisonous fly
called the Tsetse, was fatal to their aminals, especially to
the oxen, mules and horses.   This was not, however, the
only embarrassment of the expedition.   Every distant
mission has its difficulties, but the missions of Equitorial
Africa have special difficulties.   When the missioners
arrived at their destination, their trials began.   They
wrote to Archbishop Lavigerie that they had encountered
four principal obstacles—the climate, the lack of resources,
religious indifference and slavery—but with courage and
confidence in God they hoped to surmount all these.

The territory along the coast is low and marshy, and
the humidity and heat of the tropics give rise to a miasma
which produces fevers often fatal to the Europeans.   Ex-

cessive fatigue from forced marches under a burning sun, a chilliness and heavy mists during the night soon produce a slight indisposition, and finally death. The Blacks are, however, acclimated to this poisonous atmosphere. On the high lands and lofty plateaus, as on the banks of the Tanganyika, the climate is salubrious. The fertile soil produces without much cultivation wheat, beans, potatoes and manioc, which last forms the principal nourishment of the natives, The oil of the banana and the palm tree constitute the principal sources of wealth to the country.

The second difficulty is the lack of resources. " In less than three years," writes Father Lavinhac, " we have expended one hundred and fifty thousand dollars, and yet we have only arrived at the stations." This expenditure is not, however, enormous, when we consider that the Evangelical Society of London sends out each year to Protestant missions one million dollars.

The Negroes manifest an indifference towards religion, yet the assertions that certain tribes have no kind of worship and no idea of a supreme being, are false. Father Livinhac, who had been sent to Nyanza, wrote to Archbishop Lavigerie that he found in Africa the most gross idolatry, but no atheism.

At Ujiji, the principal city of Lake Tanganyika, the great evil of Africa, the Negro slave trade, is practiced in all its repulsiveness, and is the most stubborn obstacle to Christian civilization. The Arabian traders, who are aided by some Negro associates, have made this village the depot of their odious commerce. P. Deniaud depicts in striking colors the abomination of this traffic in human beings.

" The peaceful villages of the Negroes," he writes, " are suddenly surrounded during the night by these fierce adventurers, and, although the Negroes are supplied with arms, they are overpowered by men who are armed to the teeth.   All who seek shelter in the darkness of the night are captured and started on a long journey through unknown countries.   Then begin a series of unutterable miseries.   Men, women and children are forced to walk, and the strong men are bound by the hands and the feet, so that they cannot escape.   They walk all day, and when at evening they halt for a short repose, they receive a very frugal meal.   The fatigues and privations of the first days weaken a large number, especially the women and old men.   In order to terrorise this unhappy human brood, the conductors strike the exhausted Negroes a severe blow on the neck with a wooden club.   With a cry of pain they fall to the ground, and die amid agonizing convulsions. The fear of a similar treatment gives strength to the most feeble, who immediately fall into line.   Every time that a slave stops this frightful spectacle is repeated.

"When the first days of such a life have exercised their deleterious influence, a sight not less horrible awaits the victims.   The dealers in human flesh have learned by experience what the Negroes can endure, and they know at a glance those who will shortly succumb to fatigue.   In order to economize their meagre nourishment they kill them with the blow of a club.   The corpses are suspended on the branches of the neighboring trees, under which the unfortunate Blacks are obliged to eat and to sleep.   And what a sleep !   Among the young Negroes whom we rescued from this living hell and restored to liberty were many who for months afterwards would awake from sleep with a cry of horror. They were witnessing again in their dreams the bloody scenes of the captivity. The slaves march sometimes for months, but every day their number diminishes, and if in their extreme misery they attempt to revolt or escape, their ferocious masters tie them together, cut off the muscles of their arms and legs, and leave them along the roadside to perish from hunger and despair. Truly, a person might trace his way from Equatorial Africa to the villages in which the slaves are sold, by the dried human bones which line the path. And what remains at the end of the journey? Only a third or fourth part of those who had been captured.

"Then commences a much more odious scene. The captives are exposed for sale. Their hands, feet, teeth, all the members of their body are thoroughly examined. When they are sold, they belong body and soul to their master. Nothing is considered—neither the ties of blood, for they are pitilessly torn from fathers and mothers, nor their conscience, for they may be forced to embrace the religion of their Mussulman masters, nor shame itself, for they must submit to the most shameful conduct. Even their lives are at the disposal of their masters, who are held to no account for their death. It has been estimated that at least four hundred thousand Negroes have fallen victims every year to this pest. In twenty-five years, which is the average life of the Negro, the number will increase to ten millions."

It was Archbishop Lavigerie who, through the voice of his missioners and his own investigations, denounced this crime to the civilized world. But some writers of more

or less consideration, have attempted to demonstrate that
the Negro, with his brute instincts and vices is created for
slavery, and never can appreciate liberty.   This point of
view would justify a discussion on slavery, but when it is
question of the capture and the sale of the Negroes, every
political, economical and philosophical argument recedes
before the leading question of humanity.   If the Black is
not adapted for liberty as it exists amongst civilized
nations, he has an absolute right to protection.   It is the
right of the feeble against the strong, of the ignorant
against the learned, of the poor against the rich, of the
unfortunate against the favored.   He who would not
praise the lofty designs of Archbishop Lavigerie, and in
some way become associated with that great work, has
neither a humane nor a Christian heart.

Some pious laymen, formerly Papal zouaves, joined the
expedition of the missioners in order to guard the Negro
carriers.   These men represent the armed force of the
little band, a role which the priests of Jesus Christ could
not well perform.   Six armed auxiliaries accompanied the
two caravans of apostles sent out in 1879 to re-enforce
the White Fathers, who had departed the previous year.
With an inspiration which recalls the crusades and the
glorious era of the military orders, the ceremony of
departure took place in the basilica of "Our Lady of
Africa."   The Archbishop blessed this army, and each
volunteer, as an equipped knight, made his solemn pro-
testation at the foot of the altar, in these words :

"I am resolved, with God's grace, to devote myself for
one year to the mission of Equatorial Africa, and I promise
on my faith as a Christian to observe during that time all

the regulations of the auxiliaries of the mission. I promise to obey in everything the superiors of the mission to which I shall be attached, and the chief who shall be selected by the advice of the missioners. In evidence of which, placing my person under the protection of "Our Lady of Africa," I sign with my own hand this agreement, one copy of which I shall place at the feet of the miraculous statute, and the other in the hands of the superior of the African mission."

(Signed.)————

Given at "Our Lady of Africa," June 20, 1879.

CHAPTER XII.

THE WORK OF CARDINAL LAVIGERIE IN EQUATORIAL AFRICA—LAKE NYANZA.

Whilst the White Fathers at Tanganyika were establishing their abode to the north of Ujiji, in the province of Urundi, Father Livinhac and his companions had settled at Lake Nyanza, in the kingdom of Uganda. At Tanganyika, the numerous small states which are more or less frequently at war with one another, form a kind of confederation like the Swiss Republic, whilst at Nyanza the various small kingdoms are tributaries to Matesa, a powerful black prince who is sovereign of the kingdom o Uganda. This kingdom is somewhat similar to the German Empire, in which the confederate states cannot act without the formal assent of the Emperor William.

The missioners knew that their first step was to win the good will of Matesa, who was loath to recognize them.

An incident, however, shortly won his friendship. The French missioners had been forestalled by a Protestant preacher, named Mackay, who, fearful of the influence of the Catholic missioners, and actuated by a spirit of rivalry unbecoming a Christian, had prejudiced the king against them. Fortunately, Father Livinhac was endowed with a natural tact, and with that virtue of prudence, of which Archbishop Lavigerie had so highly spoken, he remembered that in a mission of North America the chief of a recently converted tribe had been won by the allurement of a red French dress, trimmed with gold lace. He knew the weakness of the savages for bright articles and brilliant colors, and consequently, before quitting France, he had gone to the market of the Temple, where the dealers of old clothes are located. "Thanks to our successive revolutions," he writes pleasantly to Archbishop Lavigerie, "I found comparatively new dresses of senators and ministers. I made a selection for king Matesa and his court. This manœuvre was very successful, and in his generosity he permitted us to preach the Gospel to his subjects, and presented to us thirty head of cattle, and a few acres of land covered with banana trees. Moreover, he furnished the material and workmen for the construction of a house for our accommodation." The reader must not think that this people, who had not a knowledge of at least the first principles of architecture, could not erect a house, for the Negro huts are not very complicated—some posts, reeds, herbs and straw—such are the materials for a building in Equatorial Africa.

It is not astonishing to read the following words of that courageous superior, Father Livinhac, to the Archbishop of Algiers : "Tell those who manifest a desire for this mission, that they must acquire a great spirit of faith which will lead them to see God in everything, and a true love for the cross which will teach them to embrace privations and trials, for the tribulations of Kabyl and the other missions convey no idea of the hardships of the missioners of Equatorial Africa." He remarked to the Director of the novitiate of Maison-Carree : "What good we could accomplish if we had amongst us a St. Francis Xavier! Fill your young men with the spirit and the zeal of that saint, and send them to us. Endeavor, by all means, to form good superiors who shall possess three leading qualities—great sanctity, great meekness and great firmness." This humble missioner was himself endowed with these qualities, and he required them for the trials which shortly would fall upon his mission.

In order to facilitate the management of the missions of Nyanza and Tanganyika, Archbishop Lavigerie founded at Zanzibar a religious house which would be the centre for communications between the novitiate at Maison-Carree and the stations of Equatorial Africa. The increase of Christians and neophytes necessitated the establishment of additional stations, and Father Livinhac repaired to Algiers to lay this question before his superior. Henceforth, two vicariates apostolic and the provicariates of Unyamwezi and the Upper Congo claimed the attention of the White Fathers. Father Livinhac was consecrated bishop of Nyanza, with the authority upon his return to the Negro country of consecrating Mgr. Charbonnier vicar-apostolic of Tanganyika ; but this consecration was retarded by the sad events which transpired in Uganda.

During the absence of Father Livinhac the mission of Rubaga had been entrusted to Father Lourdel. Matesa had died, and Mavanga, his son and heir, was first favorable to the missioners. He had been instructed in the Catholic religion, and the lords of the kingdom strongly suspected that he was a Christian, but this suspicion was groundless. His partiality towards the Mussulman slave traders gave rise to an era of persecution against the Europeans. In September, 1885, Father Lourdel accompanied the king on a journey through the kingdom, and upon their return the king was informed of the arrival of a German caravan which proposed to take possession of Bagamoyo and Usagara. His vexation was augmented by the information that Bishop Hannington, of the Anglican Missions, would shortly arrive at Uganda, by way of Massaya, and that the Anglican Missioners would meet him upon the eastern coast.

The thought of being thus encircled by Europeans gave rise to much anxiety. Besides, there was an ancient prediction that by way of Massaya the enemy would enter the kingdom of Uganda. The poor king, depressed by this sombre presentment, said to Father Lourdel : " I am the last king of Uganda, and after my death the whites will seize my country, but whilst I live I shall oppose them. With my death, terminates the line of Negro kings." This gloomy prediction was fatal to the Christians. He sent one of his own representatives with imperative orders to conduct the Anglican to the frontiers of the kingdom. Some days later he was informed that, notwithstanding his command, the whites had penetrated Uganda, and in his anger he ordered their death. The English Protestants vainly attempted to obtain the revocation of the command, and in their despair they supplicated Father Lourdel to intercede for them.   The prayers of the good priest forced from the king a promise to recall his threat, but whether he wished to deceive Father Lourdel, or whether the sentence had already been executed, Hannington and his escort of forty men were massacred.

Not content with his first victory, the king and his prime minister wished to drive from the country Mackay and two other Anglicans.   Father Lourdel was secretly informed of this move, and he immediately acquainted the three Protestants, who desirous of saving their lives, gave a magnificent present to the king, and told him that they knew of his criminal design.   Surprised at this avowal, he demanded the name of the informer, but Mackay was silent.   The king now forbade the natives to visit the houses of the whites.   Father Lourdel inquired whether this proscription applied to the Catholic missioners, and he was told that, on the contrary, they might continue the instruction of their neophytes.   Such was the state of affairs when the king was suddenly attacked by an inflammation of the eyes.   Father Lourdel applied a lotion, and in a few days the inflammation disappeared.   He ordered the royal patient to take an opium pill before retiring. During the night he was attacked by a violent nausea, which, his counsellors insisted, was the effect of the opium pill, and they advised him to imprison the priest.   In vain did one of the counsellors maintain that he himself had taken three opium pills without any evil effect.   Father Lourdel with difficulty prevailed upon the king to accept a preparation of nitric acid to counteract the nausea, for the spectators incessantly repeated : "The king is a fool to receive a remedy from the hands of a white man. He has ordered the death of the whites, and this one will seek revenge by poisoning him." In a few days, however, the king was perfectly restored, and his prejudice vanished.

Joseph Makasa, a faithful Christian and a warm friend of the missioners, ventured to say to him: "Why have you begun to kill the whites? Your father never killed them." This bold rebuke was his death sentence ; for he was condemned to be burned at the stake. Immediately all the young catechumens hastened to Father Lourdel. "The king intends to drive you away," they said, "baptize us, for we will soon be put to death." How could he refuse this touching request of future martyrs? During these days of anguish he baptized a hundred and thirty-four persons, many of whom were afterwards massacred. They were seized and tied to bundles of reeds, which were ignited, and thus they expired amid excruciating torments.

Meanwhile, Bishop Lavinhac returned, and he was filled with admiration at the heroic courage of the new Christians. "During the month which I spent at Rubaga," he writes, "not a night passed that I did not receive several Christians. I gave confirmation to seventeen. Sometimes, overcome by sleep, I attempted to take leave of my pious visitors ; but they would reply: "Stay with us, for to-morrow we shall receive from the king our death sentence, and we shall see you no more on this earth." How could I resist that appeal ? We prolonged the conversation on the vanity of worldly pleasures, and the joys of heaven which one blow of the executioner would merit for us. The future martyrs waited until morning to

receive holy Communion, and, fortified by the Bread of
Heaven, they went forth courageously to meet the trials of
the day."

The execution was followed by a pillage which almost
destroyed this flourishing Christian village. Archbishop
Lavigerie was informed of the persecution, and he appealed
to the French, Belgian, English and German governments
to use their influence with the Sultan at Zanzibar for the
cessation of the massacre; but petty rivalries paralyzed
their efforts, and nothing was done to check the bloody
caprice of a Negro king. The persecution lasted almost
one year, for in June, 1886, Father Lourdel writes thus to
the Superior of the Algerian missions :—

" *Very Reverend and dear Father Superior :*

" We no longer envy the other missions, for Uganda has
also its martyrs. Twenty of our best and most influential
neophytes have been either burnt at the stake, massacred,
or cut to pieces, whilst others have been beaten to death,
and many are yet in chains. At one time we hoped that
we ourselves would increase the army of the martyrs, but
God did not judge us worthy of this crown. The devil
has received the power to attack only those whom we have
begotten in the faith. But our hour will come, would
that it were here! Bishop Lavinhac, our reverend Vicar
Apostolic, has departed with Father Giraud for Bakumbi,
and Fathers Deniaud and Amance remain with me to
encourage and fortify our Christians in the midst of their
terrible struggle. King Mavanga does not pause in his
course. Less intelligent and more avaricious and cruel
towards strangers than was his father, he has already

sacrificed a large number of his faithful friends. His heart responds to two vibrations,—avarice and fear. He suspects everyone, whites, Arabs, and even his own subjects. The Protestants are anxious to leave, and two of them depart to-morrow. As for me, Mavanga has declared that he will never allow me to go; perhaps he will hold me as a hostage in case of an attack from the whites. We are, however, in the hands of God. Pray for us. If we must follow our neophytes to heaven, so much the better. We continue our holy ministry amongst the Christians who come to us at night. During the first year I baptised two hundred and sixty-four persons. Our orphans are studying the truths of religion, and are much attached to us."

When the victims had reached a hundred, many of whose names the superior did not even know, Father Lourdel resolved to visit the fierce persecutor, but he was given an audience only with the prime minister. He had the sad privilege of witnessing the capture and the imprisonment of a large number of young Christians. Their farewell was heroic and touching, for they had the gift of courage and of faith. The king severely reprimanded them on account of their belief, and he exclaimed in a loud and angry voice, "All those who pray, stand on this side;" and at a given signal, the executioners seized these generous confessors and led them to their death. At this touching spectacle Father Lourdel felt his very strength leave him; he was not permitted to speak one word of encouragement to his dear neophytes.

Bishop Livinhac arrived some days after this massacre. He feared to reproach the king for his crimes, lest he be

CROSSING THE SAHARA.

the innocent cause of additional cruelties; but he petitioned for boats in which to conduct some of his fathers towards the south, for he resolved to leave only two or three priests in this persecuted territory. Mavanga seemed displeased at this announcement, but he permitted the fathers to depart without, however, promising to terminate the persecution. Father Lourdel had said that "the heart of the king responded to two vibrations, avarice and fear;" and it was fear that threw him into the hands of the Christians. In 1888 the Mussulmans conspired against him and placed upon the throne his brother, Kiwewa. The partiality of the new king towards the Christians aroused the suspicion of the conspirators, who put him to death and gave the sceptre to another brother, Karema. They seized the missioners and confined both Catholic and Protestant for some time in the same prison.

During these successive revolutions, a Christian named Honorat, a former minister of Mavanga, organized an army in favor of his master, who was wandering from refuge to refuge, despised as a dethroned king, knowing not whither to turn his steps until at last he found an asylum with the Catholic missioners. The Christian army offered to espouse his cause, and on October 5th they placed again on the throne the persecutor who had shed their best blood. In his good resolutions, he wrote thus to Archbishop Lavigerie:

"I, Mavanga, King of Uganda, write to inform you of my return to my kingdom. You have doubtless heard that when the Arabs drove me from my throne, I was protected in Bugumbi by Bishop Livinhac and his missioners, who showered upon me every kindness.

Four months afterwards the Christians found my asylum, and after a struggle of five months we have triumphed over the Arabs. I supplicate you to send priests to preach the religion of Jesus Christ in the whole kingdom of Uganda. I understand that your Father, the Pope, has sent you to treat with the powers of Europe for the extermination of the slave trade in the countries of Africa. I will aid them to overthrow this commerce in human flesh in all the countries which border on Nyanza. Ask God to give me the grace to live a good life, and I beg him to bless you, and assist you in all the works you undertake for His glory.

" Your child,

" MAVANGA, King of Uganda.

" November 4, 1888."

Would that this were the termination of the history of Uganda, for it is painful for a Christian writer to add that the ruin of this fruitful mission was not the work of Mussulmans ! Bishop Livinhac, who had consecrated Mgr. Charbonnier, Bishop of Tanganyika, was forced to return to Algiers, where he was appointed Superior General of the White Fathers. When his successor, Bishop Hirt, a native of Alsace, arrived in Uganda, he found the country peaceful and prosperous, religion respected, six stations under the care of fourteen priests and three brothers, five thousand neophytes and an equal number of Christians, thirty chapels erected in the peaceful Christian centres, and the disasters of the persecution repaired. Such was the state of Nyanza after some years of labor by the White Fathers.

The blood of the martyrs had produced a fruitful harvest; but Protestant hatred, upheld by the agents of the English East-Africa Company, destroyed this beautiful picture. This company is composed of merchants, but it is exclusively Protestant, and under the control of the London Bible Society. During the disturbances which succeeded the revolution of Uganda and the dethronement of Mavanga, the Protestants had formed a distinct organization, and the very existence of this party gave birth to a Catholic party. After the return of the king, there were two camps which divided the burdens and the districts; and although the Protestant party was inferior in number, it was protected by the English fort. Fear and policy, rather than conviction, actuated Mananga in extending his protection to the Catholics, for to them he owed his restoration. He was present every Sunday with his court at the instructions, and although this conduct exasperated the Protestants, it gave him prestige in the eyes of the Catholics. The culprits who were brought before him were examined with impartiality, but when the condemnation fell upon a Protestant, he invariably appealed to the English fort, and was sustained in the face of all justice.

One day a Catholic in lawful defense killed a Protestant chief who had attacked him with a band of aggressors. Captain Lugard, of the English fort, wished to examine the proceedings, and, whilst he parlied with Mavanga apparently to obtain justice, he secretly distributed English firearms in the dead of the night to a hundred Protestant blacks. The following day, January 4, 1892, some shots to which the Catholics replied, were the signal for a

frightful struggle. On the square in which stands the
capitol a fierce combat was waged, and although there
was no proportion between the two parties, the poor
Catholics had to contend not only against the protestants
of the country, but also against the English arms.
Mavanga accompanied by two thousand Christians sought
refuge on an islet on Lake Nyanza.

What became of the missioners during this time?
They were at the mercy of the hostile army which, furious
at the flight of the king, bombarded and set fire to all the
buildings. Two children risked their lives in carrying a
last appeal of Bishop Hirt to Captain Lugard. He
hastened to the scene, and with a strong force rescued the
missioners from the flames, but he conducted them to the
fort amid the insults and jeers of the Protestants who remained masters of the field. Two days later they quitted
the fort and joined Mavanga who had sought shelter at
Buddu with the Catholics. But fifty boats loaded with
sharp-shooters hurried towards the island, and the royal
residence was riddled with bullets, and four thousand
Christians were killed. The king and Bishop Hirt escaped whilst the Catholics contended step by step for the
isle, until they were finally vanquished, seized, and conducted to the English fort. Captain Lugard informed
Mavanga at Buddu that he had given the throne of
Uganda to Maboga, the king of the Baganda Mussulmans,
on account of his partiality towards the Protestants. The
priests were taken prisoners by Captain Williams and
confined in the fort of Kampala. "What ignominy to
France," writes Father Guillermain, " to see her priests
and her children prisoners in an English fort, despised and

scoffed at by Protestant soldiers, as if they were vile criminals!"

Captain Williams informed the White Fathers that he proposed to wage a war of extermination against every Catholic. When Europe was apprised of these events there was some parleying between England and France. Captain Lugard and Williams transmitted false information to the newspapers, but Bishop Livinhac sent a refutation to the journals of Algiers, and the many letters of the White Fathers substantiated his refutation. "We might cite facts," writes one of the Fathers, "which would equal in ferocity the most odious actions of the Arab slave traders. On the island of Sesse, a Catholic named Anastasia was cruelly beheaded because she refused to accompany the Protestants who intended to enslave her. Their treatment of the Christian women and children, even with the consent and under the eyes of the English agents at Kampala, is too repulsive for repetition. Certainly were the government of the Queen informed of this conduct, these savage and licentious officers would be severely punished, for the officers of a civilized nation and the chiefs of brigands are not synonymous terms."

After having devastated Uganda by fire and by sword, the English Company was fearful of the very men whom they themselves had armed. The only resource was to welcome a second thief—the Mussulman slave-traders—whom only two years previously they were obliged to drive from the country. And now, under the pretext of terminating the conflict, the English president recalled Mavanga, and proposed to loyally divide the country with him, but this loyalty reserved for the Protestants the lion's share, and conceded a small portion to the Mussulmans and to the Catholics. All the Catholic chiefs were placed systematically on one side, and the religion of Islam became under this regime the state religion. The authority of Mavanga was nominal, for the principle that "the king reigns, but does not govern," was applied in all its force by the English Company in Uganda.

The king, yet a Catechumen, ascended the throne, but he wielded the sceptre at the cost of his faith. He persecuted his family on account of their religion, and April 3, 1892, he signed a treaty with Captains Lugard and Williams in which he consented to banish the Catholic Blacks to Buddu, with the command that they should not propagate their religion without *the authorization of the head of the English Company ;* and if they behaved well the head of the company reserved to himself the power of modifying the conditions which had been imposed upon them. This clause is in opposition to the international conventions of Berlin and Brussels, but the English wished to impress Europe with the idea that the Catholics had been the aggressors, whilst, on the contrary, they had been the victims of a vile plot.

During this frightful period the German station of Nyanza was favorable to the Catholics. "From the thousand women and children who had been exposed during the horrible revolution," writes Bishop Hirt to Lavigerie, "the head of the German station at Ukala has rescued a hundred, whom he has returned to us." Bishop Hirt returned to Rubaga with the resolution of reconstructing the ruined missions ; but what a spectacle for the heart of a Frenchman and a missioner to witness! Fifty thousand neophytes, plundered, exiled, or massacred; thousands of women and children condemned to slavery; and thirty chapels in ashes. Such was the work of English fanaticism and of the English Company of East Africa, the conquerors of Uganda.

Bishop Hirt called on Mavanga, and although the poor king had not officially espoused Protestantism, he was, nevertheless, a very submissive servant of the English of Fort Kampala. The grace of baptism had preserved the females of the place, for they were firm Catholics, notwithstanding the endeavors of the Protestant ministers to effect their apostacy. Rather than abandon their faith they informed the king that they would escape to Buddu.

In November, 1892, Captain Macdonald, a delegate of the Queen, was sent to investigate the cause of the Catholic persecution at Uganda. He was accompanied by M. Volf, a German traveler, from whom he obtained accurate information of the recent occurrences. He saw at Buddu the results of the persecution and of the hatred of his co-religionists—the most abject poverty, misery and despair; for the poor Blacks had lost their homes, their wives and their children, and thickly congregated in the marshy places, they became an easy prey to fever and the other maladies which are so prevalent in that country. Bishop Hirt wrote, in 1893, that of the one hundred thousand neophytes who were at Buddu the previous year, one-half had perished. As the result of the investigation of the delegation the Catholics of Uganda were given two new provinces and the island of Sesse. This was a tardy and incomplete reparation. May the day come when entire justice will be given.

The mission of Tanganyika had not to contend with the English protestants, but with serpents and wild beasts, enemies more easily avoided. The arrival of Bishop Charbonnier amongst the poor Negroes was an important event. The orphanage of Kibanga had more than one hundred restless Negro boys, gathered from all parts of the country, and we may well imagine the welcome of Bishop Charbonnier amongst this curious class. There were many adventures at Tanganyika, but what were they in comparison to the persecutions of Nyanza? Father Guilleme, who accompanied the bishop to Kibanga, remarked in a letter to the Superior at Algiers: "Of all the enemies of the plains of Kibanga, the most formidable are the tigers. Lately they have destroyed twenty-eight of our goats, and although for three nights we have placed a goat as a decoy, we have not captured the enemy."

Bishop Charbonnier died at Karema, shortly after his arrival, on the sixteenth of April, 1888. Bishop Bridoux, his successor, had just terminated his pastoral visit when he, too, succumbed to fever and died at the age of thirty-eight. He had visited the village of Saint Louis of Merumbi, founded by Captain Joubert, and he gives evidence of the great faith and piety which he witnessed. "This village," he says, "is constructed partly of wood and partly of brick. The noble Captain directs the constructions, governs this little world, attends to the sick, presides at the morning and the evening prayers and at catechism." This village is several miles from Lake Tanganyika, and the bishop promised to send, as soon as possible, missioners who would take charge of the spiritual affairs. Archbishop Lavigere had the pleasure of having one of the missions called after him. "At Lavigerieville," writes Bishop Bridoux, "the Christians are very numerous, but it is necessary to transport the village to the neighboring hill, for the retreat of the lake has formed marshes which, with all our efforts, we are unable to render healthy. The death rate amongst the children is such that we should not recoil before this expense, great though it be." The zealous bishop was unable to effect this formidable move, for he died after having evidenced the success of Captain Joubert in organizing the Negro tribes of the region for the resistance of the slave trade.

Amongst the Arab slavers whom Bishop Bridoux met were Tippu-Tib, of whom Stanley speaks in his work, *In Darkest Africa*, and Romaliza, who was proudly entitled "The Sultan of Tanganyika." "Tippu-Tib impressed me most favorably," writes the bishop, "his sympathetic reception was, indeed, an enigma to which we shortly found the key. The fierce and insolent Romaliza, who, in his ambition to exterminate the Negro tribes, has been the cause of so much bloodshed and destruction, knelt at my feet and supplicated me to recommend him to Emin-Pasha. The soubriquet of 'Romaliza' indicates in one word his vile character; it signifies 'he who kills,' and it was constantly upon his lips. If he sent brigands against the Blacks, he gave them the command, 'maliza,' kill them; if the conquered chiefs were brought before him, his answer was 'maliza'; if his subjects captured an insufficient number of elephants, he replied, 'maliza'; when he wished to war against Captain Joubert, his instructions were: 'Treat with him, capture him, and then—maliza, kill him.'"

Since the Congress of Brussels, and the crusade of the European governments against slavery, the wolf seemed converted into a lamb ; but he was simply restrained by fear.   It is with slaves as with other prohibited merchandise, recourse is had to smuggling.   Tippu-Tib personally renounced the slave trade, but he had under his command Arabs and half-breeds who pursued the traffic.   Romaliza failed to dispose of the slaves whom he had captured in his last invasion, and he offered some hundred children to Bishop Bridoux for a nominal sum of money.   The good bishop eagerly accepted the proposition—his last act of charity towards this unfortunate people, for he died shortly afterwards.

The premature ruin of the missions was doubly deplorable, for, owing to the revolutions and the invasions of the Mussulman slave-traders, there was no possible route to Equatorial Africa.   After the destruction of the Christian kingdom of Uganda, Archbishop Lavigerie sent Father Deguerry to attempt a new entrance by Zambesi.   His efforts were successful, and a new station was established with the permission of the king of Portugal at Lake Nyassa, and by this route the caravans afterwards proceeded.   Emin-Pasha has testified to the devotion and the labor of the zealous missioners.   He wrote from Victoria Nyanza, in 1891 : " During my sojourn I frequently visited the Catholic missioners from Algiers.   I was on terms of intimacy with them, and I was shown the most attentive hospitality. There is a singular contrast between the Protestant and the Catholic missioners.   The Catholics labor seriously to make the Negroes intelligent and useful, whilst the Protestants sing hymns and feed them to satiety.   If we wish the best results, we should by all means procure the labors of the Catholic missioners, and supply them with the means of elevating the Negro." Certainly, this testimony is beyond dispute, and with these encouraging words we shall close our remarks on these distant missions. It is time to return to the Algerian colony and follow the many patriotic and Christian undertakings of Archbishop Lavigerie.

CHAPTER XIII.

ARCHBISHOP LAVIGERIE IN TUNIS.

We last saw Archbishop Lavigerie chagrined at the death of his first missioners, and at the hostility of the French deputies in withholding the state appropriations for religious works, but neither sadness nor hostility could dampen his zeal. These mental and physical fatigues, however, had impaired his health, which was never robust, for he had inherited rheumatic affections which had prematurely carried off his family. The strain of incessant labors forced him to apply for a coadjutor, and his increasing debility led him to seek a few weeks of rest in Europe.

The time seemed propitious for this temporary absence, for he had succeeded in regulating the affairs of the church of Constantine, which under the administration of Bishop Las Casas had become financially embarassed. The Bishop of Constantine, more zealous than prudent, had erected many religious buildings, and had encumbered the diocese with the enormous debt of two hundred

and twenty-five thousand dollars, but through the kindness of Admiral de Gueydon and of the government this
debt was liquidated, and the responsibility of the diocese
was entrusted to the Vicar General of Viviers, Mgr.
Roberts, who was consecrated by his coadjutor in the
Cathedral of Algiers.   The Archbishop entrusted to Mgr.
Soubiranne, the Bishop of Sebaste and late director of the
" Schools of the East," the administration of the diocese
during his absence ; but his health declined so rapidly
that he feared he might not materialize a project which he
had long contemplated.

He felt that now he might renounce his dignities and
the honors of the episcopacy for the life of the simple
missioner of the order of the White Fathers.   " My dear
children," he wrote to his sons in the beginning of 1872,
" my conscience will not allow me to send you alone into
the perilous arena.   Amongst your number are many
whom I have sent afar into the battle-field to seek the
crown of martyrdom.   I cannot choose their successors
unless I myself give them the example in generosity.
You have left all in response to my appeal ; I have sacrificed nothing, for I still retain my episcopal see.   This
thought tortures me.   He is not a general who leads not
his army, nor he a shepherd who flees at the approach of
the wolf.   I have besieged heaven with my prayers, and
my declining health seems to me an indication of God's
will.   With the permission of the Sovereign Pontiff I
shall exchange my archiepiscopal see for your habit and
rule, that I may become one with you in life and in death."

Fortunately the Pope would not listen to this untimely
appeal, for he knew too well that the duty of a general,

except in case of emergency, is not to expose his life in the heat of the battle, but to protect and direct his troops, to point the way, and from his post of observation to spur them to victory. Pius XI was moved even to tears at the request of the Archbishop, but he commanded him to continue the government of his diocese, the burden of which was lightened by the appointment of Mgr. Duserre as bishop of Constantine and coadjutor-bishop of Algiers.

The apostolic zeal of Archbishop Lavigerie was shortly satisfied, for Providence opened to him a territory on the borders of Algeria, and his memory will be forever associated with the history of Catholic Tunis. This province has a coast line of about fifteen hundred miles extending from Tubarkha to the Gulf of Cades, and a surface of about half that of Italy. It is bound on the east by Tripoli, on the south by the Sahara Desert, on the west by the Algerian possessions, and on the north by the Mediterranean Sea.

Every classical scholar is familiar with the political history of Carthage, the rival of Rome ; and the victories of Scipio and the ruin of the country of Hannibal from part of the historical education of every child. But the modern destiny of that illustrious republic which Archbishop Lavigerie longed to make a Christian State, may not be so well known. Tunis received the word of God from the Roman converts, and it is a pious tradition that St. Peter visited Africa. The gospel spread rapidly, and in the second century a council of sixty-six bishops convened at Carthage. That famous city had for seven centuries many renowned pontiffs, doctors and martyrs, amongst whom were St. Fulgentius, Tertullian, Cyprian, Perpetua,

Felicitas, Monica and Augustine. The barbarian and Arabian invasions under the Calif Omar in 643 erected the Mussulman kingdom on the ruins of Christianity, for although Africa had her saints, the corruption and heresy of many Christians had drawn down this terrible chastisement. Soon the only faithful in Tunis were the victims of piracy, snatched by the Corsairs, Turks and apostates from the shores of Sicily, Corsica, Sardinia, Italy, Provence and Spain. Thus, St. Vincent de Paul, a martyr to his heroic charity, was loaded with chains and condemned to the galleys of Beylick.

Deprived of all religious consolation, these Christian victims erected altars in the obscure corners of the galleys, and there the sons of St. Vincent de Paul and of St. Francis strove amid the most extreme peril to exercise their ministry. This continued until the conquest of Algiers in 1830. The presence of the French troops intimidated the Arabs and enabled the Italian Capuchins to establish several parishes in Tunis. In 1842, the Superior, Mgr. Suter, was appointed Vicar General of the province. When this pious prelate had attained the age of eighty-four, he supplicated Pope Pius IX to allow him to retire from active life, but his prayer was not heard. An unforseen expedition, however, gave a new turn to the vicariate apostolic of Tunis. French and Italian influence had been for some time antagonistic, and the Bey, Metaspha-Ben-Ismael, had been circumvented by M. Maccio, the Italian consul, who had insulted M. Roustan, the French minister. The depredations of the Kourmirs gave Roustan an opportunity of interposing with an armed force, and the Bey, perceiving his mistake at having espoused the cause of the Italian, was forced to submit to the protectorate of France.

Mgr. Suter had proposed to the Holy See the names of three Italian subjects from whom to select his successor, but the French government demanded a French bishop. There was only one man who could amalgamate the heterogeneous elements of Tunis—Archbishop Lavigerie—and by a decree of June 28, 1881, he was appointed apostolic administrator of Tunis, with the request that he bestow an annuity on the aged Italian bishop. The French government, which had refused to extend a credit to Algiers, now resolved, even against the desire of the deputies, to sustain the Archbishop. They authorized a lottery, which realized two hundred and fifty thousand dollars, but the Archbishop had expended eight hundred and seventy-five thousand dollars—he had thrown himself energetically into the work—schools, hospitals, churches, religious establishments and asylums were immediately erected. M. Maccio, the Italian agent, paid a tribute to his activity and zeal: "Ah, Archbishop," said he one day, "what good you are accomplishing in Tunis! But how that good reflects on us."

In fact, the very presence of the Archbishop was more effective than an army. The village of Sfax had resisted the French expedition, and after a severe bombardment it was captured, and the inhabitants condemned to pay a large indemnity. Archbishop Lavigerie came as a messenger of peace, bearing in his hand the olive branch. "He was welcomed by the people as a prince," writes Mgr. Lesur; "a regiment of soldiers formed his body guard, the cannon fired a military salute, the citizens appeared in holiday attire in expectation of a great event. He gave two thousand five hundred dollars to the church, which had been severely damaged by the bombardment, and he distributed abundant alms to Christians, Jews, and Mussulmans alike. Public rumor soon made known this kindness, and the inhabitants were profuse in their thanks."

"When he departed from the church he was overwhelmed with demonstrations of gratitude, and on his arrival at the Presbetry he was met by Mussulmans, who desired an interview. They pictured to him their deplorable condition, for on the following day they would have to pay the indemnity of the war unless the great priest of the Christians aided them. In consideration of the great audience, the Archbishop, attired in his pontifical robes, repaired to the church accompanied by the terrified Mussulmans. He ascended the steps of the altar and stood before them in all the grandeur of his dignity. He impressed upon them the malice of their offence in despising the authority of their sovereign ; Sfax had previously manifested a seditious spirit, and their present conduct had aggravated their crime. As a Catholic Bishop, his mission was one of mercy, but the manifestation of mercy implied the deep repentance of the inhabitants, otherwise it would be a weakness and not a virtue. "Do you repent?" he asked. "Yes ;" they replied, "we have done wrong ; the Bey is our master, France is strong and we are weak." "But," he added, "your old chief, Ali-Ben-Khalifa, says that you have promised him to revolt in the springtime." "It is false," they indignantly replied, "we have been his victims ; we do not wish to revolt." "Well, then," said the Bishop, "swear to me that you will never rebel against

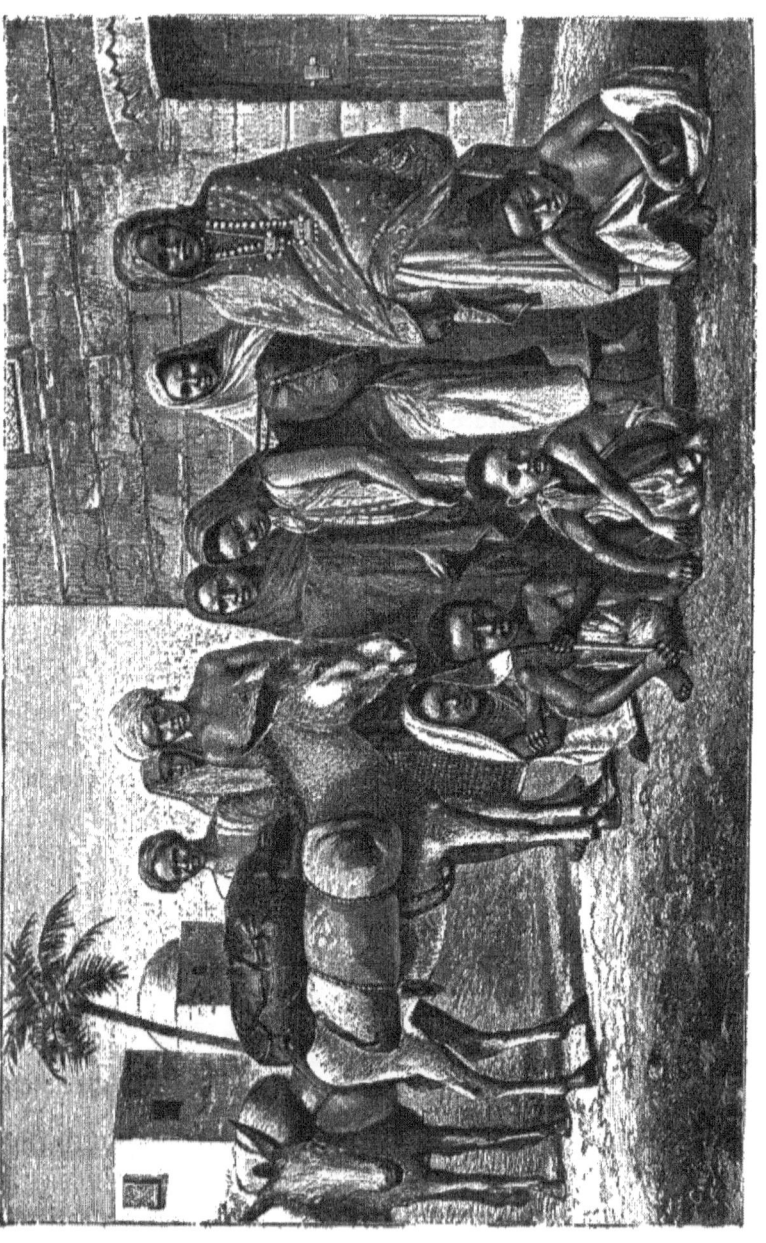

A FAMILY GATHERING—NEAR THE EQUATOR.

your lawful sovereign, the Bey, nor against France, his ally and protector." "We swear, as God sees us," they cried. "On this condition only will I exert my influence," concluded the Bishop. "What do you wish?" They desired sufficient time in which to fulfill their obligation, for they could not then procure the money. Their houses and lands would have to be mortgaged, and this could not be accomplished immediately."

"The Archbishop reassured them of the consideration of the Bey and of the representative of France, but he insisted on their fidelity in cancelling as soon as possible this sacred debt. The government kindly granted his request, and the indemnity was faithfully paid. That evening the village was magnificently illuminated in honor of the distinguished visitor, and amid the general rejoicing the Jews and Mussulmans were most conspicuous. On the following day the enthusiasm was so intense that the inhabitants detached the horses from the Archbishop's carriage and carried it through the streets amid the cheers and blessings of the spectators."

Although he was influential in a political point of view, he saw clearly that the interests of religion would not progress. In Tunis, more than elsewhere, many remnants of Christianity exist. Polygamy is found only amongst the wealthy, who are of Turkish origin. The natives are not nomadic; they dwell in stone houses and cultivate the soil, and are less fanatic than other Mussulmans; but although some tribes have as a traditional remembrance the sign of the Cross tattooed on their hands, face and arms, the present generation is so filled with the prejudices and superstition of the Coran, that the organization of missions such as exist in other infidel countries, would be fruitless. The only elements of zeal in the estimation of the Archbishop were the education of the young and charity and good example to all. Instruction and works of charity constitute the mission of priests and religious, but good example is the vocation of every one, and that living sermon would, in the course of time, dissipate all the false religious sentiments of the sons of Islam.

The Mussulmans interpret the zeal and the devotion of the Catholic priests after their own fashion. "You priests," they say, "are enlightened by God; you consider yourselves Christians, and in the depth of your heart you are, but you will be true believers, *i. e.*, sons of Mahomet, when you die." There is a strange tradition regarding St. Louis, of France, who died in Carthage. The Mussulmans ardently admired his many virtues, and they claim that at the hour of his death Mahomet appeared to him, and carried his soul to heaven, and some even place him in the catalogue of their saints.

The Archbishop in his ardor and zeal for the spread of religion pursued the plan which he had adopted in Algiers, of populating Tunis with French Catholics. He felt that this country offered advantages superior even to those of Algeria. He wrote in 1885: "I wish to afford to the old families of France an opportunity for labor and useful investment, and by this means make some return for the many kindnesses which they have showered upon me. That I ask no sacrifices, you may judge for yourselves. When the French occupied Tunis, the best land sold for ten to fifteen dollars an acre. In less than three years the value has rapidly increased, and a definitive value has not yet been reached. In Algeria the irrigated lands of the plains vary from one hundred and twenty-five to one hundred and fifty dollars an acre, whilst in the villages and neighborhood of Algiers, the garden lands watered only by wells have advanced as high as one thousand and fifty dollars an acre. But in Tunis the best land in the neighborhood of the villages does not exceed forty dollars an acre, whilst in the south, towards Sfax and the Gulf of Cades, it is as low as ten dollars an acre. You see then the advantages for men of fortune, who in the unsettled condition of Europe cannot securely invest their money. Not to speak of the new industries, particularly the cultivation of the grape, the simple superior value of the land will become in time a source of wealth. Others will follow the pioneers, and if they be honest Christians, they will have my hearty encouragement. That which preoccupies me as pastor of the province, is not, however, the financial and ecomomic question. I see in the advent of such proprietors and colonists the accomplishment of the great work which we shall effect by our very presence." Thus again did the Archbishop of Algiers promote the interests of the Church and of France ; and the Church in manifestation of her gratitude conferred upon him one of her highest dignities.

CHAPTER XIV.

ARCHBISHOP LAVIGERIE CREATED CARDINAL — HIS WEALTH — HIS ANTI-COLONIAL POLICY.

During the pontificate of Pope Pius IX there was question of conferring upon Archbishop Lavigerie the cardinal's

cap, but Marshal MacMahon sat in the presidential chair
of France, and the former governor-general of Algeria had
not forgotten his encounter with the Archbishop. Notwithstanding his indisputable military abilities and his
private virtues, he was obstinate in his antipathies.
Grandeur of soul often presents a counterpart of petty
weaknesses ; and the old soldier, inflated with his past
victories, had not forgiven the defeat which he had suffered
from Lavigerie and the Arabian orphanages. But, in 1882,
this obstacle no longer existed, and M. Grevy was not a
personal enemy of the Archbishop.

There was universal joy in the colony when this great
honor was conferred upon their Archbishop. He had,
with a truly patriotic sentiment, reconstructed the chapel
upon the spot where King Louis IX had died, and there
it was Count Cecchini presented to him the cardinal's cap.
The ceremony was the occasion of a manifestation of love
and esteem towards the new cardinal, but in his humble
piety he felt obliged to abase himself in proportion as his
worldly glory increased. The Maltese detached his horses
from the carriage, and much to his discomfort and chagrin,
carried him in triumph through the streets. When he
arrived at the church, he cried out : "I am only a man,
and it is not becoming to render me such honors." His
reply to Count Cecchini was grave and serious : "It is as
dean of the French bishops that I have been recommended
to the Sovereign Pontiff. The many years of my episcopal
ministry and the fatigues of the African climate will soon
convert the purple into a shroud. In the presence of such
a spectacle, what other sentiment can fill my soul than my
own weakness and misery ? Of myself, I am nothing, but

the Church which sends me gives me the assurance of God's support. The designs of Providence seem to indicate that Carthage, subjugated by the pagan Romans and barbarians, shall be restored to life by Christian Rome."

This utterance betrayed the secret desire of the Cardinal for the restoration of the See of St. Cyprian, which had been dead for a thousand years. He referred to this in his letter of gratitude to Pope Leo XIII : "When I shall have endowed the Vicariate of Tunis with every requisite in institutions, missions and resources, the happiest day of my life will be that on which I shall cast myself at the feet of your Holiness, and beg you to restore the See of St. Cyprian, and revive the great church of Carthage." Four years later this pious desire was accomplished, for on January 25, 1886, Leo XIII re-established this famous See, and a superb cathedral sprang up under the magic touch of the Cardinal. It was a mixture of Moorish, Byzantine, Gothic and Roman styles. The white basilica, surmounted with a dome, the lofty spires and the great golden cross overlooked the city of Tunis, the entire gulf, the mountains of Ariana, Cape Bon and the distant ruins of Utica.

On the day of the consecration, the decorated arches, supported by two hundred colonnades of Carrara marble, presented a most pleasing spectacle. The Cardinal was second to none in the arrangement for a religious feast; not a detail escaped him. He ordered and arranged everything. Twelve bishops were present in their episcopal robes and added splendor to the occasion. The first Archbishop of new Carthage, in all the pomp which the Church permits to her pontiffs, appeared in the very spot where the last bishop of ancient Carthage had been insulted, beaten with clubs and cast into prison. He spared no pains in the entertainment of his guests. He had often been falsely accused of a weakness for pomp and ceremony. Personally, he was opposed to luxury and expense; he lived a simple, unostentatious life, in close imitation of the White Fathers. But he had lofty ideas of the manner of conducting a feast, a reception or a ceremony. Nothing was too good for God, for the majesty of his worship, and for the dignity of a representative of the Church and of France. Then he was lavish and regardless of expenditure. Those who admired him and saw the extent of his works, were profuse in their generosity. But his new dignity, far from impeding his flights of zeal, confirmed his vocation as a mendicant friar, and the obstacles which retarded others only stimulated his ardor.

At the beginning of 1886, a severe attack of a chronic malady brought him to the verge of the grave. He had received the last Sacraments and had entrusted the administration of the diocese of Algiers to his coadjutor, P. Degurry, when contrary to all expectation he suddenly recovered. He was convalescing, and obliged to take the utmost precaution and repose, when the deputies, again forgetful of his services, suppressed the credit intended for Algeria. This was the blow of the lash which brought him to his feet. He immediately dispatched a letter to Paris to the director of the "Schools of the East." "Tell your associates that I shall set sail for France. I am coming to extend my hand for the love of God and of France. My health is feeble and my strength nigh exhausted, but I prefer to die of fatigue on the highway, than to die of shame at my hesitation and weakness at a time when the French clergy of Africa are persecuted." The impartial historian will some day contrast the miserable declaimers who thought that they protected the financial interests of the nation and the noble mendicant who hastened to France in the interest of those institutions which are the pride and the honor of the Church and of France.

To the shame of the members of the French chamber, they heartlessly and unjustly cut off the appropriation, and public charity was again destined to sustain these grand undertakings. Europe assumed a generous spirit in the presence of the Cardinal, pressed down by the burden which weighed heavily upon his shoulders. It was necessary to provide for his numerous institutions, a few of which we may mention. An apostolic school of five hundred children ; a novitiate for sixty persons ; five establishments under the sisters ; a hospital for natives ; and eight other institutions in Algiers ; a scholastic and a new cathedral at Carthage ; a French college, a bishopric with its chapel, a seminary and French parochial schools in Tunis ; a college for Greeks in Jerusalem ; a college for young Negroes of the interior of Africa at Malta ; eleven establishments in Equatorial Africa ; preparatory seminaries in Rome, Paris and Belgium ; four apostolic vicariates, any one of which was capable of absorbing the entire resources of the Cardinal. These were the principal effects of his zeal, and for which millions of dollars were not sufficient.

The natives considered him immensely wealthy. One day his brother, Felix Lavigerie, an officer of the army, entered a cigar store, and as the Cardinal was passing in a

hired carriage, the proprietor said to the officer: "Do
you wish to see the richest man in Algeria? Look, there
he goes." "What is his name?" asked the officer. "The
Archbishop of Algiers." "Indeed! And is he so very
rich?" continued Felix. "Yes," said the merchant, "he
cannot count his wealth. He owns all the land on either
side of the railway from Algiers to Oran, and all the vessels in the harbor." "Why," replied the officer, wonder-
fully amused at this remark, "I thought these vessels
belonged to a well-known company." "Oh, yes," added
the merchant, "they do in name, but the Archbishop
really owns them." "What does he do with the money?"
asked Felix. "Why, he enriches his family." This was
too much for the officer, so he made no effort to remove
the false impression. A gentleman who had defended the
Cardinal's reputation against a similar charge received a
letter of thanks through a local paper. The Cardinal
enumerated his various possessions, and terminated thus:
"Such are my millions, which in fact are neither millions
nor mine. A financier who cannot balance his books is on
the verge of ruin. I am that financier." He could only
say that the immense amounts which passed through his
hands were not his own. In order to assure the continuance of his works he gave to the Society of the White
Fathers all the property which he had acquired, but they
were not enriched by this donation, which was encumbered
with numerous mortgages.

The Cardinal was in his sixty-fifth year when the action
of the French chamber obliged him to begin again a sub-
scription tour throughout Europe. France is a country of
contrasts. Side by side with a majority of the electors

who represent the nation at the Bourbon Palace and who joyfully suppressed the donation to the national clergy, were a generous and enthusiastic multitude who willingly opened their purse strings to the venerable Cardinal. At Rennes, after a short address in the cathedral, he received three thousand six hundred dollars, and at Paris, Bayonne, and in the entire south, he was welcomed with an enthusiasm which compensated him for the injustice of the French authorities.

In the meantime the French government, impressed by the general movement, established a credit of twenty thousand dollars in favor of the Algerian clergy. This paltry reparation of a suppression of one hundred and fifteen thousand dollars given annually to the three dioceses of Algiers, Constantine and Oran, was debated before the chamber of Deputies and was twice defeated. Ashamed of an action which rendered France odious and ridiculous in the eyes of the natives and the colonists, the Cardinal, in the name of the bishops of Algeria, boldly refused this pittance, which would only call down on the French clergy humiliating discussions. So the appropriation was withheld, and the Cardinal supplicated alms rather than accept the offer of a sovereign of Europe who proposed to support the seminaries which supplied apostles for Equatorial Africa, on the condition that the flag of his nation be raised over these institutions. " The Cross of Christ is the only standard of the Apostles," replied the Cardinal, " yet I thank you for your generous proposal ; but to a Frenchman, next to the Cross comes the standard of France." We can easily understand the motive which prompted this offer. The missioners had opened through Uganda a road

to commerce and to civilization.   King Matesa had
wished to place his kingdom under the protection of·
France, and had the officers of the government seconded
the views of the great Frenchman, France might to-day
rule over an empire in Africa equal to the English possessions.   But the Deputies by their anti-religious policy had
developed to their detriment an anti-French and anti-
colonial policy.

CHAPTER XV.

CARDINAL LAVIGERIE AND ANTI-SLAVERY.

On the 24th of May, 1888, Cardinal Lavigerie arrived
in Rome with Algerian pilgrims, whom he presented to
the Holy Father, Leo XIII, who was then preoccupied
with the question of slavery.   The accounts of the explorers
and the letters of missioners were filled with the details of
the inhuman treatment inflicted upon the unfortunate
Negroes.   He had just addressed a letter to the bishops of
Brazil in which he insisted on the united efforts of the
Brazilian clergy for the extermination of that social leprosy.

Stanley, who may be suspected of neither tenderness
nor compassion towards the Negroes, says that "one
hundred Negroes are destroyed in order to procure two
slaves.   The traders burn the huts, kill the first inhabitants
whom they meet, and surround the others, from whom
they select only the most profitable.   The villages disap-
pear as if they had only existed in the imagination."

Father Guilleme writes the following letter to the Cardinal :   " I saw a drove of slaves in Ujiji—long files of
men, women and children ; some with ropes around their

necks, others bound together by a rope which pierced their ear. I met at every step living skeletons who could scarcely walk, even with the aid of a cane; they were not bound, because they were no longer able to escape. Suffering and privations were depicted upon their emaciated countenances; the victims were dying rather of hunger than of disease. Gaping scars upon their backs manifested too clearly the cruelty of their masters, who forced them to continue their journey under the sting of the lash. Others lay starving on the streets, awaiting patiently the end of their miserable existence. A young Christian, ignorant of the roads, wished to go to the border of the lake, but he recoiled with horror at the sight of the numerous corpses, half-devoured by hyenas and birds of prey. He asked an Arab why these corpses were so numerous in the neighborhood of Ujiji. ' We are accustomed,' replied the Arab, indifferently, ' to cast there the carcasses of our slaves, but this year the number of deaths has been so large that the animals have been gorged with human flesh.'"

Two vessels freighted with slaves were captured at Zanzibar by the English cruisers. Mgr. Bridoux describes the scene : "Twenty-four slaves were crowded into a narrow passage not large enough to hold ten. Their emaciated bodies and sunken eyes pictured too plainly their cruel treatment. A more horrifying sight cannot be imagined than those miserable wretches, covered with sores, wearing on their hands, arms and neck the marks of the cruel lash."

Among the Algerian pilgrims whom Cardinal Lavigerie presented to the Holy Father were two young Negroes whom the White Fathers had snatched from slavery. Leo XIII again expressed his compassion for these poor slaves—a compassion which should find an echo in the heart of every Christian. He was loud in his praise of the devoted missioners who endeavored to repair the evil, and he terminated with these words: " But to you, Cardinal, we are indebted for the success of this work. We know what you have done, and we are confident you will not cease until you have brought this great undertaking to a happy ending."

The Pope's wish was for Cardinal Lavigerie a command. Old and and feeble though he was, his energy was capable of overcoming any obstacle. He must undertake a new crusade ; he must travel through Europe, organize committees, collect alms, obtain the coöperation of the governments, and place at the head of this permanent international congress a man capable of concentrating the authority and mode of action. A young prelate, Mgr. Bruncot, the Procurator of the African Missions, had attracted his attention, and he enlisted him as his coadjutor. Filled with hope, and convinced of the justice of his cause, he set out with his purse and staff. Paris was the first to receive the revelation of the courageous Cardinal. His account of the horrors of the slave traffic touched every heart and opened every purse. His passionate eloquence was magnetic. At every meeting he organized the best and wealthiest men of Paris into anti-slavery societies. A council of personages high in standing, under the presidency of Jules Simon, was invested with the duty of defending the cause of abolition amongst the political and national assemblies, the learned bodies and the newspapers.

From Paris he went to London. He was received by Cardinal Manning and Lord Granville with courtesy, but with, perhaps, that instinctive mistrust which England entertains towards French colonial questions. But his first discourse aroused the sympathy of all. His glowing. tribute to the memory of Livingstone immediately enlisted the attention of his Protestant hearers. An anti-slavery society was organized, and some days later the president, Sir Sidney Buxton, obtained from the government permission to induce the king of Belgium to take the initiative for a congress at Brussels. The Cardinal's arrival in Brussels assumed the importance of a political and religious event, for the king was the first to propose the extinction of slavery by force of arms. After the first lecture five thousand dollars were donated, and five hundred young men placed themselves at his disposal for the defence of the Blacks of the Upper Congo.

The Cardinal wished to visit Germany, Spain and Portugal, but his declining health rendered this journey impossible. He, however, appealed to these countries, and societies were rapidly organized, and in Spain the Queen Regent was pleased to become the protectress of the work. But the prospect in Italy was not bright, for, as he was suspected of having influenced Tunis in accepting the protectorate of France, his presence was neither agreeable nor desirable. Even the clergy manifested hostility, and the Italian Capuchins whom he had driven from Tunis shared in the national antipathy. However, his prestige as Archbishop of Algiers won for him a respectful and even a generous welcome. In Milan, he recalled the memory of St. Augustine, who belonged to Italy through

his intimate relations with the holy Bishop Ambrose. The
enthusiasm of the Neapolitans was intense. The Archbishop of Naples had received a magnificent pectoral cross,
valued at two thousand dollars, a testimonial from the city
for his exertions during the cholera epidemic. In his
generosity he gave this cross, studded with precious gems,
to the Cardinal, who, however, had too much delicacy to
accept a sacrifice which might wound the feelings of those
generous Catholic hearts.

This constant labor told on the constitution of the Cardinal, and he arrived in Algiers in a state of such exhaustion that he was compelled by his physicians to pass the
winter at Biskra, on the borders of the desert. In his
European tour he had not visited Switzerland. This
country seemed a suitable place for the international congress; so, in August, 1889, he summoned all the committees to meet at Luzern. The city was jubilant over the
prospect of such illustrious and benevolent guests; and for
two weeks before the opening of the congress every room
in the hotels was engaged. The Cardinal arrived some
days in advance to seek a much-needed rest on the shores
of the lake. The condition of his health became so serious that at the last moment he was obliged to postpone
the congress. Many openly accused him of fickleness and
caprice, but those who knew the deliberation with which
he always acted, saw a more profound motive in his conduct. It was patriotism. He was informed that the influential members of the French anti-slavery committee could
not respond to the summons, for they were in the heat of
an electional campaign. He feared that in the absence of
a majority favorable to France, the international assembly

might propose certain measures inimical to the plans of his country. Rather than oppose the interests of France, he preferred to be branded as fanatical and fickle.

The following year, 1890, he convoked the international congress at Paris, and every nation was represented. There were also present at the opening Bishop Livinhac, the courageous missioner who suffered in Uganda for the true faith ; young Negroes who intended to follow the course of medicine and of theology at the college of Malta, and an escort of White Fathers who had accompanied the Cardinal on his tour through Europe. Their very presence made a profound impression on the spectators. The congress was preceded by a conference of the plenipotentiaries who had participated in the preliminaries for the congress of Brussels. The questions relative to the slave traffic were so elucidated that three meetings were sufficient in Paris to draw up the important resolutions. This stamped with the seal of a methodic organization the great work of the Cardinal. The congress expressed its gratitude to all the committee, and desired the immediate enforcement of the resolutions.

The anti-slavery movement was composed of national committees which were morally united, but absolutely independent in their mode of operation. The congress advised each committee to labor in its own provinces ; thus France in the Sahara, Dahomey, the Soudan and the Congo. Measures should be taken to secure freedom for the Blacks and fidelity to the promises which were made to them. It called the attention of the powers to the danger of sectional strifes, which would paralyze all efforts for the civilization and freedom of the Negro tribes.

One more organization was needed to complete the work. The Brothers of the Sahara, those generous volunteers who, in imitation of Lieutenant Joubert, would teach the Negroes the system of self-defence against the attacks of their assassins. The Cardinal established for this purpose a novitiate at Biskra, where the armed Brothers might learn the language of the tribes on the outposts of Dahomey. They received a special training in agriculture, medicine, the fertilization and development of the oases of the desert.

Such was the establishment and the progress of the crusade which he had preached, of whom Jules Simon writes in a Protestant journal : " Cardinal Lavigerie ! A man of this generation whose name will ·be enscribed in indelible characters on the pages of history." And we may repeat with him that this great man drew the inspiration of his grandeur, not from the maxims of this world, but from the lofty principles of the Gospel. He constantly respected and gave expression to the noble emblem which was enscribed upon his arms, an emblem which may be expressed in one word, " charitas," charity.

CHAPTER XVI.

THE EPISCOPAL JUBILEE — AN HISTORICAL TOAST.

On the morning of March 22, 1888, the Cathedral of Algiers appeared resplendent with decorations; everywhere were garlands and festoons, gold and purple tapestry. The walls were concealed under heavy foliage and

A NATIVE PRIEST.

Algerian flowers, which formed in immense letters the following inscription :

"Charles Martial Lavigerie, Cardinal of the Holy Roman Church, Archbishop of Carthage and Algiers, Primate of Africa, who, by his rare services to Africa has enrolled his name amongst those who merit the highest praise from the Church and from civilization.

"LEO XIII, *Pope.*"

These words were taken from a letter recently addressed to the Cardinal, and this celebration was the 25th anniversary of his elevation to the episcopacy. On the previous evening the parish bells of the neighborhood rang out the joyous announcement. The Cardinal seldom resided at the archiepiscopal residence, but in the preparatory seminary of Saint Eugene, near the cathedral of "Our Lady of Africa." A throne was erected in the court of the archiepiscopal residence, and before the celebration of the mass, the prelates, vested in mitre, cross, and cope, assembled to offer their congratulations to his Eminence. The papal nuncio at Paris had sent as his representative a prelate of the palace of his holiness, Leo XIII. All the bishops of Africa, the representatives from the Patriarchs of Antioch, Alexandria, and Jerusalem, and many officers of the government were present.

When the Cardinal ascended his throne Mgr. Duserre, the Archbishop of Damascus and coadjutor of Algiers, presented to him the offerings of the clergy—a pectoral cross, a ring studded with diamonds, and a beautifully bound album, in which were the congratulations of the priests and the religious of Northern Africa. After the ceremony numerous other gifts were presented, amongst which were a massive gold chalice, another pectoral cross, a mitre, ornaments and sacred vases for the poor churches of his diocese. The Cardinal was moved to tears at this spontaneous manifestation of the love and attachment of his faithful subjects, and this weakness touched the spectators more than could the most eloquent address. After the first moment of emotion he expressed his sincere thanks, and then taking his ring from his finger, he offered it to his coadjutor, saying : " You have, in the name of my faithful clergy, presented me with a new ring. I wish you to possess after my death the ring which I wear to-day. Allow me to present it to you. I ask only one favor ; when my hand will be cold in death, and yours will be raised in benediction over my children, remember that beyond the grave I, too, will love them and will bless them." When the Cardinal entered the cathedral a choir of two hundred voices intoned the " Ecce sacerdos magnus," and all were spell-bound under the charm of that grave and religious music of Haydn, which expressed so beautifully the sentiments of every heart.

The Cardinal had intended to pass the day in silence and recollection, but he acceded to the request of the Sisters of Charity to speak in favor of the poor of Algiers. On his way to the convent he desired to visit the shrine of "Our Lady of Africa." What was his astonishment to see grouped around this holy sanctuary the Christian Arabian families of the two villages of Saint Cyprian and Saint Monica, which he himself had founded. The Arabs presented to him his grandchildren, as they called them; and the dignified, serious and ceremonious Cardinal had the weakness of a grandfather towards these Arabian children. The contrast was the more striking, because generally he assumed in the presence of his visitors and guests a majestic air which sometimes disconcerted even his own household. For although he might manifest a lively and jovial manner towards them, yet by a word or a look he could teach them their position. It was not a rare thing to see his vicar-general and his canons preserve a respectful and prudent silence in his presence. But the children and the unfortunate were certain of a warm welcome. He had founded at Attafs an orphanage for deserted Arabian children, and he frequently visited this institution. Sometimes the children would climb upon his knees and run their hands through his pockets in search of sweet-meats. "I am filled with joy," he exclaimed one day, "when I think of the goodness of God, who, in his boundless charity, has preserved these innocent creatures and showered upon them the graces of Christianity."

After receiving the congratulations of the young Arabs at the shrine, he conducted his guests to Saint Eugene, where a splendid repast had been prepared. Mgr. Averardi, who occupied the place of honor as the representative of the Holy See, presented the congratulations of Leo XIII to the venerable Cardinal. A magnificent illumination terminated this beautiful day, in which he had reached the zenith of human glory. As Jules Simon had well said, "He was a man for whom the age had the highest honor and respect. The Pope esteemed him as a brother; the crowned heads as an equal; the Catholic world as an apostle; his enemies as a lofty patriot."

The Pope was to entrust to him a work which would confirm his patriotism, even at the risk of sacrificing the noble African undertaking.   In October, 1890, he went to Rome in the interests of anti-slavery.   He found Leo XIII agitated and preoccupied over the tendency of the Old World, and especially of Christian France.   The modest outlines of this simple biography cannot embrace the history of the successive revolutions which, during the present century, have spread over France.   Everyone is acquainted with the party strifes which were the outcome of the hatreds and sympathies arising from dynastic quarrels—sentiments often worthy of respect, inasmuch as they represent the chivalrous and legendary fidelity of the Frenchman of the *old regime* to God and the king, but prejudicial to the welfare of a country, when, through detestation of the republic, they withdraw honest and intelligent men from public affairs.   The republican government has much that is blamable, and its movements since 1881 explain sufficiently the passionate attacks and profound antipathies against it ; for to many men, lacking neither intelligence nor attachment to country, the word republic is synonymous with irreligion, injustice and financial disorder ; and the actions of the government have too often verified this figure of speech.   The fault lies with associating the actions of the republican government with the republic itself.   Thus the ground of contention has been shifted.   Instead of struggling for a principle, or for the protection of a religious or a national interest, the attack has been directed against a personality or a form of government.   This policy is the material and moral ruin of a country ; and France has been the victim of such a policy for almost a hundred years.

Leo XIII, with that eagle eye which sees beyond worldly interests and petty rivalries, deplored this state of affairs, and resolved to intervene. The Church is opposed to no form of government; consequently, they who desire to serve the cause of Catholicity must not confound it with the political cause. Moreover, they must, irrespective of party, unite for the energetic defence of religious interests. They must accept the republic as the lawful government, and endeavor to obtain from it the liberty of the Church in the exercise of her providential mission. Were the Church to espouse the cause of the fallen dynasties, she would be an enemy to the republic.

Such were the expressions of the Pope to the Cardinal, and such was the line of conduct which his Holiness desired the clergy and the French Catholics to follow. He requested the Cardinal to take the initiative in France, for he was the most conspicuous member of the Catholic hierarchy, and his word would carry with it great weight. The Cardinal's postition was most perplexing. His great and beautiful work depended partly on the charity of those Catholics whose opinions, prejudices and sentiments of chivalrous fidelity he was asked to overthrow. He respectfully mentioned this difficulty to the head of the Church, who immediately replied: "When a father expresses his desires to his sons, secondary considerations are of little conseqence."

The Cardinal detailed to Bishop Livinhac, the venerable Superior of the White Fathers, the ideas of the Pope and the disastrous consequences to them and to the African Missions. The Bishop simply replied: "The Pope asks it. We cannot refuse what is for the good of

the Church, even if we be buried under our own ruins."
He had heard the desire of the Pope and the approval of
the Superior of the African Missions ; there remained only
the opportunity of publicly manifesting to France the
mind of Leo XIII.

On the following month, November 12th, 1890, he
invited to a banquet at the Archiepiscopal residence of
Saint Eugene, the staff of the squadron of the Mediterranean, the vice-admirals Duperre and Alquiner, the rear-
admirals O'Neil and Auger-Dufresne, and forty officers,
besides many officials of the government. At the end of
the repast, he arose amid a respectful and profound
silence and proposed the following toast :

"Gentlemen—Allow me, before our departure, to drink
to the health of the French navy, so nobly represented
here to-day. Our navy recalls many glorious and endear-
ing remembrances of Algiers. From the first day the
navy aided in the conquest, and the name of the eminent
man who commands the squadron of the Mediterranean
brings back as a distant echo the first song of victory. I
am happy, Admiral, to pay my respects to those who
represent in Algiers the authority of France, to the heads
of our valiant army, our administration and our magis-
tracy. What touches me most tenderly is that you have
all assembled at the invitation of an aged Archbishop,
who, in order to promote the interests of France, has
made Africa his native country. May that same union
which binds us together soon reign in the hearts of the
sons of our mother country. In the presence of the bloody
past and the threatening future, union is our supreme
need. Union is, permit me to say, the first desire of the

pastors of the Church in every grade of the hierarchy. That Church asks us to renounce neither the remembrance of the glorious past nor the sentiments of fidelity and gratitude which are honorable in all men. But when the will of the people is clearly defined, when the form of government has nothing contradictory to the principles which can christianize and civilize nations, then absolute adherence to this form of government is necessary to preserve it from the threatening abyss. The moment is come to terminate these dissensions, and to sacrifice whatever conscience and honor will permit. That is what I uphold, and what I wish the clergy in France in every rank to uphold; and in this desire I am confident of the approval of every authorized voice. Without this resignation and patriotic acceptance, order and peace are overthrown, social and religious destruction are imminent. Those who wish to accomplish their work of folly give to our enemies a spectacle of our ambitions or of our hatreds, and fill the heart of France with that discouragement which is the precursor of final catastrophies. The French navy and army have set the example. They have maintained their ancient traditions, whilst they remained true to their national standard under whatever form of government it was furled. This is one of the causes of the respect and honor which the French navy wins wherever it unfolds its flag as a symbol of pride to the name of France. Allow a Cardinal missioner to say with all gratitude and thanks, that it has nobly protected the Christian missions. Gentlemen, I drink to the French navy."

Admiral Duperre then responded: "I thank your Eminence in the name of the French navy, to which you

have paid such glowing tributes.   I drink to the Apostle
of Africa and to the clergy of Algeria." Some hours
later the reporters telegraphed the news over Europe, and
on the following day the public papers were in an uproar.
The Cardinal's expectations were fully realized.   The
Radicals, who were enemies of the Church and of her
ministers, termed him ambitious ; the Catholic Conserva-
tives branded him as a deserter.   Those who qualified him
as ambitious, could not clearly indicate his motives ; for
at that moment, through his personal worth, he was, next
to the Pope, the most influential prelate of Christendom,
and, consequently, the accusation was groundless. Although
the Catholic Conservative journals were respectful towards
his personality, they attacked with energy his declaration.
But impartial history will make due allowance for them,
for they were ignorant of the part which the Holy Father
played in this extraordinary step, and, notwithstanding the
significant remark of the Cardinal—" I am confident of the
approval of every authorized voice "—they did not know
with absolute certainty that he had been only the mouth-
piece of Leo XIII.

The majority of the journalists, whose exasperation
drew from them excessive terms of exaggeration, made no
distinction between the republic itself and its misdeeds.
" Yes," said one journal, " the trial has been made ; but
great God ! what a trial !   The Christian religion banished
from all the primary schools, the public manifestation of
worship interdicted in the large cities, the Sisters of Charity
driven from the hospitals of Paris, the clergy debarred
from the bureaus of charity, Catholics practically excluded
from all civil, judicial and administrative functions, social

atheism recognized by law, so that from the time of the first magistrate of the republic, no one dare mention in public the name of God; and there is no hope of a material change in the dispositions of the dominant party." "When the hand of destiny," said another paper, "shall demand an account for all the misdeeds, follies and demoralization caused by the republic, I am firmly convinced that the tears which the Empire has cost France will be insignificant in comparison to the tears which the present republic will cost. Had I not this firm conviction, I would be a republican; but I am as fixed in my horror for the republic as the Arab in his love for the Coran. All the music of the White Fathers will never convert me."

This is only a faint echo of the utterances of many journals. Some French bishops accepted the views of the Cardinal, but many preserved a respectful silence through regard for him rather than from conviction. The toast of the Cardinal had not diminished the utility of his undertakings, but the alms for the missions were considerably diminished. The discontent of the enemies had its effect upon the poor Negro slaves. Charity and enthusiasm for the anti-slavery movement were withdrawn, and the extremists momentarily withheld their sympathy. But happily the wise utterances of the Sovereign Pontiff and the effect of the election appeased French Catholics, and posterity will render justice to the filial submission and the purity of intention of the Cardinal Archbishop of Algiers.

CHAPTER XVII.

A PEN SKETCH OF CARDINAL LAVIGERIE.

Before we recount the last days of the great Frenchman we may pause a moment in the contemplation of that noble character whom the Holy See so justly appreciated and whom France so differently understood.   In the opinion of his adversaries and of his admirers Cardinal Lavigerie possessed superior faculties.   No one was better fitted than he to guide and direct mankind.   He was endowed with the genius of a commander, and with all the exceptional qualities and resources which made him an incomparable leader.   He seemed to grasp at a glance all the details of an undertaking, the best method of realizing it, and the result.   This foresight never failed him in his various enterprises, and often proved both a help and an obstacle. We have seen that even as a seminarian and a young priest he was not understood, and during his long career his opponents often collided with the angles of his incomparable superiority.   In an inferior position he would have found material for discussion, but in the first rank no one presumed to control or oppose his actions.

His appearance was rather that of a general than of a bishop.   His orders were absolute.   He admitted neither discussion, observation nor the slightest delay in the execution of his commands.   He alone knew the motives which actuated him, and his suborninates had only to obey his orders.   His manifold occupations explain sufficiently his conduct. He had neither the time nor the taste for the indulgence of parliamentary rules, and he would no more allow his vicars-general or his missioners to question his orders than a commander would permit a simple soldier to advance the least theory in opposition to his commands. Obedience seemed to him the only virtue which could preserve discipline and bring to a happy termination the works which he had undertaken.

Even the excess of his qualities raised him above the ordinary. In any position he would have evinced a lofty character and a powerful personality. Providence had selected him as the light of the French hierarchy, but his talents, character, energy and genius as a ruler and an organizer, would have made him a great man in any other career. As a soldier, he would have with Rostopchin set fire to Moscow to save his country the humiliation of a foreign occupation ; as a diplomat, he would have with Talleyrand at the congress of Vienna, preserved to France amid the ruin of war and revolution, the prestige of a powerful nation ; in a word, he would have shone as a leader, and we may say without fear of contradiction, he would have been a perfect president of that ideal republic which two years before his death he had publicly espoused.

In the presence of such rare and commanding qualities, we can easily understand that sweetness, forbearance and condescension were not his dominant virtues. Were he of a hesitating and vacillating disposition he never would have accomplished such stupendous undertakings ; and if sometimes his admirers were stung by a too harsh manner, they could never doubt the goodness of his heart. We speak of the Cardinal's admirers, but not of his friends.

The reason is plain. Friendship implies confidence, similarity of tastes and views; in a word, sympathy and an equality of subjects. Cardinal Lavigerie had no equal. He acted as a superior towards inferiors, as a father towards a son, and in Algiers, as a sovereign towards his subjects. And in this exceptional position, notwithstanding the goodness of his heart, he elicited admiration and esteem, rather than love and intimate friendship. He knew how to be simple, kind and amiable, but on the least occasion he quickly assumed his superiority. He was generous to excess; of that race of noble minds who prefer to give than to receive. Old age and its accompanying infirmities, touched a sympathetic chord in his heart, and filled him with a longing for companionship. And what nature has not this weakness for sympathy? Even our Lord in the garden of Gethsemane sought the support and the companionship of His three apostles, and in the bitterness of His heart at their indifference, He remarked, "Could you not watch with Me one hour?"

Although to his last hour the Cardinal was engaged in works which absorbed his time, his heart was ever open to the poor, the children and the unfortunate Arabs. The orphans revered him, and they have treasured many happy traits of his kind and affectionate nature. In Tunis he was esteemed even as a legendary hero. Father Beauron narrates that in the establishment of the White Fathers at St. Louis of Carthage are seen three pictures of the Cardinal in the company of St. Louis. One represents him in the act of blessing the saint before his departure for the crusade; the other as sending him to battle, and the third in the act of administering the Last Sacraments to the dying king. This glaring anachronism proves one thing—the place which the Cardinal held in the thoughts and hearts of his spiritual children.

It is said with much truth that a man is not great in the eyes of his valet, but it may be added that the Cardinal has falsified this proverb. He had the rare disposition of impressing alike his immediate subjects and those who saw him through the brilliancy and the renown of his reputation. He was a man who accomplished whatever he undertook. Goethe says: "Only in what a man does, in what he continues to do, and persists in doing, can he show character;" and in this sense never was there a firmer and more consistent man than Cardinal Lavigerie, who illustrated by his own example that nothing is impossible to an energetic and powerful intelligence. When he became bishop of Nancy he deeply regretted his ignorance of the German language, for he was unable to communicate his thoughts to the German portion of his diocese. Before his first pastoral visit he learned sufficient German to compose and memorize three short discourses. He recited them to his vicar-general, who, fearful of failure, endeavored to dissuade him from a step which might provoke ridicule and laughter. "I am equal to the attempt," replied the bishop, "but you may make me laugh; stand then behind the altar and we shall see what will happen." When he arrived at the first German village he ascended the altar-steps and began with much difficulty, but with a tone of conviction: "It is with a feeling of great joy that I come to you. I regret only my inability to speak your beautiful language." Instead of the laughter which the vicar-general had predicted, the bishop saw tears of joy fill

the eyes of his audience. Deeply touched at this manifestation, he turned towards the altar and said to the vicar-
general : " Now you may come out; for if you do not, I
shall be forced to laugh at you ; " and he continued his
discourse amid the most respectful silence and attention.
This simple anecdote illustrates the care with which he
accomplished his undertakings.

In the course of his career, which was too brilliant not
to arouse jealousy and criticism, he was sometimes
accused of ambition ; and truly he was ambitious. He
had a noble and generous ambition of utilizing every
possible means for the good of all. He saw only the end
towards which he directed his energy, and this end never
was his own personality.

He was not a writer in the strict sense of the term. He
wrote clearly and energetically ; for his writings, as his
speech, were precise, pointed, never commonplace nor
studied. He spoke well, because his thoughts were
forcible ; and when he touched upon his favorite work,
his ardent convictions burst forth with animation and
brilliancy. There was a lack of empty phrases and high-
sounding words, for he sought to instruct and convince,
rather than to please. He spoke the Latin language with
astonishing fluency. At the age of sixty-seven, he
dictated, without notes, the convocation of the Council of
Carthage and the decrees for the consideration of the
Fathers. His application of the texts of Scripture was a
spiritual commentary in itself. His thorough knowledge
of the religious history of ancient Africa was manifested
upon many occasions. This happy union of talents and
literary qualities inspired his admirers with the hope of

securing him a membership in the French Academy ; and in 1884, the secretary, with whom he had previously corresponded, invited him to present his name to the Institute. The Cardinal replied that he could not solicit the votes of the members according to the established rules. His excuse is so lofty and delicately expressed that we give it in full :

To the Secretary of the French Academy :

" In consequence of my recent illness, I have been unable to reply to your kind communication except by telegram. I wish to-day to supply for the laconic style of my answer, and to express my gratitude to the members of your Academy who have taken the initiative in my candidacy. I desire to explain my reserve, which may perhaps be a surprise to you.

" I know that the candidates are obliged to personally solicit the votes of the Academy. Two reasons deter me from this step. The first is the absence of any titles of distinction which might justify my application. I have only my good will, and when it is question of science and of positive results, good will is not a sufficient recommendation. The second is of a more delicate nature. I am only a missioner, and my other titles are insignificant. Hence, if as a missioner, I gave up all, I cannot now solicit the distinction which you offer me. I have sent a legion of missioners to break down the bulwarks of idolatry and superstition. In the strife eleven have lost their lives and others succumb to fatigue and disease. What would they say if, whilst they seek only the crown of martyrdom, I were to wear the laurels of the Institute ?

The very expression of this thought deters me. Were I
to yield to this seductive temptation, I would be covered
with shame.   It is not compatible with the life of a missioner, so I beg to remain with my barbarians.   Although
I cannot petition this honor, I and my noble missioners
will always labor with you for the diffusion of knowledge
and science, and in the service of our country."

Someone asked him one day if he were willing to become
a member of the French Academy.   He replied: " Yes, if
I do not have to make personal application ; " but he immediately added, " I would like to know who my prede-
cessor was.   I might succeed the comic writer who has
just died ; and what could I say in his praise ?   I wish
only one seat—that of M. de Lesseps, for he separates the
continents, whilst I try to unite them."

CHAPTER XVIII.

THE END OF A GREAT CAREER—FUNERAL OF CARDINAL LAVIGERIE.

During the years 1891 and 1892, Cardinal Lavigerie
suffered intensely, but the intervals of relief he devoted
assiduously to his numerous works.   He read his many
letters every morning, and as his right hand was partially
paralyzed, he dictated his replies to his secretaries. "With
the care of so many undertakings upon his hands," says
Father Kline, " he was the most laborious and generally
the least envied man on the continent.   The vicar-general,
in whom he placed the most confidence, was literally
overwhelmed with labor, and his only repose and vacation

was when suddenly dispatched upon some important mission to Tunis, Rome, Paris or Brussels."

In the month of May, 1891, whilst the Cardinal was in Tunis, he was prostrated with inflammation of the lungs. He received the Last Sacrament, and although his physician despaired of his recovery, he rallied sufficiently to be conveyed to one of the oases of the Sahara, where the mildness of the climate greatly strengthened him. He resolved to accept the invitation of Bishop Roberts to spend some weeks of repose at Marseilles, but he was dissuaded from undertaking this journey, and he soon perceived that his day for traveling had passed. He returned to his residence at St. Eugene, in Algiers, where nigh to the Cathedral of "Our Lady of Africa," he desired to prepare for that great journey into eternity.

He had at this time some difficulty with the "Armed Brothers" of the Sahara. Father Delaterre, the Archdeacon of Carthage, laid the question before him on the 23d of December, and after mature deliberation he disbanded them.

He had resolved to go to Biskra with the hope of finding relief in the dryness of that climate, but the following morning he was prostrated. He sent hurriedly for Father Delaterre, to whom he said : " This time it is the approach of death."

We cannot improve upon the words of one of his faithful sons who has described the last hours of the great Cardinal : " His Eminence was no longer able to ascend the steps of the altar, but he did not wish to be deprived of the fruits of the Holy·Sacrifice. Every morning one of his secretaries offered up the Mass in the adjoining room and brought to him the Holy Eucharist. After his thanksgiving on Thursday, November 24th, two brothers clothed him, but his paralysis had so increased that they were obliged to place him upon his couch. He could scarcely speak, although he retained perfect consciousness. A calm sleep succeeded the first violent attack, and his attendants had every hope that his strong constitution would triumph. But on Friday morning about one o'clock he manifested marked symptoms of congestion of the brain. He received Extreme Unction with sentiments of profound piety. After the reception of the Sacrament of the dying, he slept a short while, but his sleep was followed by a lethargy which lasted all day. At half after ten in the morning the venerable invalid slowly and calmly entered into his agony.

"Towards midnight Bishop Duserre began the prayers for the dying, after which he arose, and taking the hand of the Cardinal, he said in a voice trembling with emotion: "My friends, kiss for the last time this hand which has so often called down the blessing of heaven on you;" and he bowed down and he respectfully kissed that right hand already cold in death. All the attendants approached in turn, and performed this last duty of filial piety. Some moments later his Eminence, the great Cardinal Lavigerie, rendered his sublime soul to his Creator, and hastened to receive the recompense for the many labors which he had undertaken for the glory of God, for the honor of the Church, and for the salvation of the poor unbelievers of Africa. Thus passed away the venerable Cardinal in the peace of the Lord, at the age of sixty-seven years and twenty-seven days."

The news of his death cast a gloom over the Catholic world. Every party knelt before the coffin of the great Frenchman. The journals were unanimous in his praise. They all admired his broad intelligence, and bowed down before his lofty patriotism. But the highest praise came from the lips of the Sovereign Pontiff, who, through the Prefect of the Propaganda, the eminent Cardinal Ledochowski, sent a letter to Mgr. Tournier, the vicar-general of Algiers, in which he spoke in the most flattering terms of the energetic laborer of the Lord's vineyard. He terminated with this expressive remark : " His heroic labors and cruel trials have broken his physical forces and ruined his health. He fell on the battlefield, a valiant champion in the struggle of truth against error. The missioners of Algiers have lost in him a devoted father, the priests of Algiers and Carthage an experienced pastor, and the entire African church a valiant primate. For me, owing to the great affection which bound me to the deceased, I share the deep sorrow in which the Sacred Congregation is buried at the loss of a faithful co-laborer. Amid my bitter grief at the death of so eminent a person, I earnestly beg God to assist us with His holy grace, and to teach us to walk in the footsteps of the late Archbishop of Algiers."

A solemn service for the repose of the deceased in the church of St. Louis of the French, in which he had been consecrated bishop, gave evidence of the esteem of the church and of France. Similar services were held in many dioceses, particularly in Bayonne, the birthplace of the illustrious Cardinal; at Paris, where he had been elevated to the priesthood and whose pulpits he had so often electrified by his brilliant eloquence ; at Lyons, whose abundant charity had so generously responded to his appeals.

In erecting the magnificent basilica of " St. Louis of Carthage," the great Cardinal had prepared a place for his remains under the main altar. On the evening of the consecration of the church he went with the seminarians and the scholastics to this hallowed spot, which he himself desired to bless. This ceremony called forth a train of thoughts which he expressed to his select audience : " I would hesitate to sadden you by this ceremony," he said, " did I not see in it an occasion for serious consideration. God has given me the grace of keeping every day before my eyes the thought of death, and my declining health has made this thought familiar to me. And as the years increase and the supreme moment approaches, that thought dominates over all others. I have always found in it two great advantages which the Holy Ghost Himself teaches us. The first is to learn from death how to live. ' Remember thy last end and thou shalt never sin.' The other is to labor whilst we have the opportunity. ' I must work the works of Him that sent Me whilst it is day ; the night cometh when no man can work.' Thus it is that I come to this tomb to-day that I may here learn how to employ the remainder of my days in useful labor. I will come some day, not for a moment, but forever. Then will I need your prayers, for I will have to render an account of my administration to my Supreme Judge. I have wished my grave to be in your midst that you might remember your father and implore the mercy of God for him. This I humbly ask in return for my paternal love, for my fatigues and my labors : ' Have mercy on me, at least you, my friends.' " And to-day his pious request was fulfilled.

But before entrusting the remains to their last resting-place the Algerians desire to bestow special honors on him whom they considered the father of the colony. The vicar-general has described the scene in a letter to the Bishop of Autun : " I cannot presume in these hasty lines," he writes, " to give you an adequate idea of the magnificence of the display, for display it was, although it was the solemn obsequies of the Cardinal. Sadness and sorrow were lost in the unanimous admiration of public sympathy. The government had ordered exceptional honors for the Archbishop of Algiers and Carthage. The command of the authorities at Paris harmonized with the universal sentiment of the people. The office began at eight o'clock at the cathedral. Under a golden canopy in the centre of the choir rested the coffin on a catafalque. Bishops and priests were lined around the remains, and in the nave of the church were the civil and the military authorities. The Bishop of Constantine celebrated the mass, and the music was that simple liturgical chant which, when rendered by five hundred trained voices, had a most powerful and penetrating effect. I doubt if the old mosque, which fifty years ago was transformed into a church, had ever witnessed so beautiful a ceremony.

"After the mass the celebrant ascended the pulpit. He voiced the grief and the homage of admiration and gratitude of the Algerians. He spoke as a pontiff, he wept as a son, and his words, authoritative and tender, found a response in every heart. Then followed the customary absolutions. The clear voice of the Bishop sang out the

'Kyrie Eleison, Christe Eleison.' For the illustrious
and the ignoble alike, for the rich and for the poor, for
all who have crossed the channel of death and stand
before the judgment-seat of God, that prayer is opportune.
The prayers of the faithful ascend to the Master, who
scrutinizes the innermost movements of the conscience ;
they supplicate Him to be merciful to the soul which stands
before His tribunal.

"During the holy office, the guard was drawn up along
the principal streets, from the residence of the Archbishop
to the magnificent quay of the Republic. Delegations of
children, headed by their pastors, lead the procession.
Then came in turn the White Fathers, in their picturesque
costume, the clergy and bishops, the Admiral of the
squadron of Toulon, the generals of divisions, with their
staffs, four Arabian chiefs arrayed in their white cloaks,
the hearse, drawn by eight horses caparisoned in black,
Mgr. Duserre and his attendants, the Governor of
Algeria, the consuls of the different nations, the officials
of the civil and the judicial courts, the professors and
deans of the colleges, and even rabbis and Mahometan
priests.

"This imposing procession moved slowly and sadly to
the music of the military band, or the solemn chant of the
'Miserere,' sung at intervals by the clergy. An immense
throng of people crowded the streets, the balconies of the
houses and the quay. I am unable to describe the appearance and the recollection of this cosmopolitan public. I
have never seen anything so edifying. Not a loud word
broke the silence of the sorrowing spectators ; and when
the hearse appeared, every head was uncovered and bowed

in respect to their former friend and father. And that immense audience was composed of representatives from every country of Europe, not to mention the many Arabian tribes who came to manifest their respect for their savior. During twenty-five years, the name of Cardinal Lavigerie had been heard so often in Algeria that it seemed encircled with a kind of legendary admiration. Everyone knew his passionate love for France and for Africa, and his noble exertions for the advance of civilization and of religion. Many who were present might find it impossible to state the number of his undertakings, but they knew that certain honors were due to him who had so increased the honor of their country.

"At the quay the cortege was given to the admiralty to convey to the cruiser 'Cosmao,' which had been sent the day before from Toulon to bear the remains from Tunis to Carthage. When the coffin was lowered from the hearse and placed on board a launch, the Governor of Algeria advanced to the midst of the bishops and assistants, and in a voice sincerely agitated by his feelings, he said: 'I cannot part from this man whom France to-day honors, without a word of adieu. The Cardinal has wished his body to be borne to Carthage, but he has left his heart here. Here it was he began and continued the great work of his life. When no one thought of Africa, he wished to gain it for France and for civilization. He was a noble Frenchman and a brave European, the precursor of those hardy voyagers, mariners and soldiers who have realized the glory of conquerors of the New World. He struggled during his entire life, and God only knows the sorrow and the bitterness which were his lot. He was born for action,

and his life rested not on his origin, but on his destiny.
He was kind and tender to those whom he loved—passionate in his affections; and he possessed the power of
infusing into all the magnetic force of his own ardor.
His memory will ever remain sacred to France, for he was
one of her most noble children.' ..

"The remains were then carried to the cruiser by a
launch which the marine service had kindly placed at the
disposal of the Cardinal's friends.   Other boats followed
with the bishops, clergy, military and civil authorities.
When the signal was given the flotilla advanced towards
the 'Cosmao.'   The thunder of the cannon of the Admiralty and of the cruiser resounded over the waters.   The
flags of the fort were unfurled, and hundreds of boats,
ladened with saddened citizens, followed in the wake of
the launch.   The remains were slowly raised into the
cruiser, and the bishops and the attendants ascended.

"The Bishop of Constantine advanced to the side and
chanted the last absolution : 'Eternal rest give unto him,
O Lord ; and let perpetual light shine upon him.'   What
a beautiful prayer, on the calm bosom of the waters, in
sight of that city and of those mountains which the great
Cardinal had loved, and where he had labored for the
glory of God and the advancement of religion.

"Eternal rest give unto him, O Lord!   Eternal repose
to that indefatigable apostle, to that noble laborer, to that
intrepid soldier!   His earthly remains entered the hospitable shelter of Tunis and Carthage, but his pure soul
enters the blessed abode of heaven forever.

"Under the shadow of the Cross and the French standard, the body of the great Frenchman arrived at Carthage, and was religiously interred in the tomb which he himself had selected and blessed ; and the spot is marked by a marble slab on which is the following inscription :

" Here peacefully reposes, in the hope of the Infinite mercy, he who was Charles Martial Allemand Lavigerie, Cardinal priest of the Holy Roman Church, Archbishop of Carthage and Algiers, and Primate of Africa, now reduced to ashes. Pray for him."

" Now reduced to ashes." What eloquence in these words ! After the enumeration of his titles and dignities and all his human grandeur, could he better paraphrase the utterance of King Solomon : " Vanity of vanities, and all is vanity." He is now reduced to ashes ; he, the great man, the noble Frenchman, the grand Cardinal ; but he enjoys immortality in the continuance of his work. His was a life in accordance with God's will. It was a finished life, a life with a lofty purpose which he strove to fulfill. Well may we say that the world is better because Cardinal Lavigerie lived. He will never die in the remembrance and in the affections of his noble priests, his devoted people, and his bereaved Arabian children, and as they advance in the perfection of those truths which he labored to implant in their hearts, so shall he enjoy with ever-increasing glory the eternity of heaven.